To those who never fail to see the hope in humanity.

WHAT'S LEFT
BEHIND

stories from the end of the world

NICOLE A. SCHROEDER

LOST LIBRARY
P R E S S

Cover artwork by Daniel Schroeder.
Interior artwork by Abby Blenk.

Part I: What's Lost

Doomsday

*T*HE WORLD STOPPED THREE *months ago, as I stood outside your apartment, looking up at the orange glow from your window while your voice replayed in my head. Above, shooting stars peppered the night sky—a rare sight in the middle of the city. But I didn't care about any of that.*

A few minutes before, I'd been up there with you, in the same place I now watched your shadow pacing back and forth.

The room had felt stuffy, and far too warm, amid the flurry of words we threw at each other. I don't even remember now what started it this time. But it didn't matter anymore what started it; it was always the same argument in the end.

The train stopped for the third time between stations, and I fought the urge to grumble aloud in the packed car. I was going to be late to work again, thanks to the construction on the line and the growing number of tourists hoping for a chance to see the meteorological light show that had become a nightly occurrence in London over the past few weeks. I'd even left my flat fifteen minutes ahead of usual. The collar of my shirt was growing itchy and damp against my skin from the heat of so many bodies pressed together, and I shifted my weight from one foot to the other to try to distract myself.

Left *my* flat. Not ours, like we'd always planned.

The memory of that night drew the air even tighter around me, and I took in a breath, tasting the sourness of the stuffy car. It felt as if the oxygen had dissipated before it reached my lungs for how little it helped. I closed my eyes, rested my forehead against the metal handhold I was pressed against . . . But then the floor jostled beneath me, everyone swaying backward into one another and then forward again, and a brief blast of air dulled the suffocating feeling into a slight headache.

The Central line was one of the oldest and deepest lines on the London Underground, which meant it was sweltering on even the coldest days of the year. Unfortunately, it was also the only one that followed the route to the office, so I was left with no choice every day but to deal with the sweaty stink and the seemingly constant repairs. The crowded cars, with commuters packed together so tightly it felt almost intimate, was an inevitability on any line at 8 in the morning. But now that we were moving again, the squeal of the train on the track added to the overwhelm, drowning out the muffled announcements on the crackling speakers and, thankfully this morning, my thoughts.

I kept my eyes closed as we pulled into the station, deliberately turning my thoughts to the number of stops I had left. Two more until I would get off at Bond Street, then another few minutes' walk until I'd make it to work. All around me, I could feel people shuffling their way through the crowd to be the first off the Tube, then the new group of people jostling for position before the doors closed again. It was the same chaos I'd relied on for the past several weeks to make things feel normal without you.

But as the doors hissed closed and a muffled announcement played in time with the sound, something else happened that was decidedly *not* normal.

A sudden chorus of chimes, buzzes, and dings filled the train car, the sounds overlapping with one another and shaking everyone from their early morning stupor. I opened my eyes, my own phone vibrating against my leg from inside my pocket, and wore the same frown as everyone else in the car as I dug for it.

A few of the faces around me shifted from confusion to horror staring at their devices as I finally brought mine to my face.

EMERGENCY ALERT ISSUED BY THE UK GOV-
ERNMENT: IMPACT PREDICTED. TAKE SHEL-
TER IMMEDIATELY. THIS IS NOT A DRILL.

I read the message four or five times before the words started to make sense. Even then, I glanced up at the rest of the people in the car, scanning their faces, their reactions, to see if they'd received the alert, too, and if they'd interpreted it the same way I had.

They had.

For a moment, it was as if the world had stopped. We were all silent, our gazes roving around the train as we locked eyes with one another. We all wore the same expression—eyes wide, faces pale. We reread the messages, just to be sure we hadn't imagined them.

But then the moment passed. The train slowed as it began to pull into the next station, and we realized the world was still spinning—at least for now.

Suddenly, I felt bodies shoving past me, every person slamming into another as people rushed the doors to the car. Before the train had even stopped, a few people were working their fingers into the space between them, try-ing to pry them free. Without knowing what I was do-ing, and half caught up in the crush of people, I elbowed my way forward as well, pouring out onto the platform.

7

From there, the crowd split; some stumbled farther into the station, as deep underground as they could go, but the rest trampled one another in an attempt to get up to the surface. I was a fish caught up in the current around me, but the glimpses I had of other people showed me that they'd received the message, too. No one had the mind to try to understand it, to wonder what the scientists said about where it had come from or whether we'd known about it before now or what the global impact would be. No one thought logically.

We just ran.

As I tumbled out of the station and onto the street, it took me a moment to orient myself. I'd followed the same route for years, stood on this street more times than I could count, yet I couldn't seem to think. The chaos had changed this to a different world than the one I'd known, and I didn't recognize any of it. All I saw was the woman sobbing into her phone to my right, the father scooping his daughter into his arms, her princess backpack still on her back and bouncing against his arm as he sprinted down the sidewalk and shoved past me into the entrance to the station. Then the world tipped, the pavement rushing up to meet me. A shooting pain traveled through my palms and along my side as I caught my fall, scraping against the cement, and something else hammered into my back before a woman fell over top of me, landing hard on her shoulder. I reached a hand out to help her, but she didn't even notice, pulling herself to her feet and running in the same direction she had before, her jacket sleeve dangling down to her elbow. I scrambled to my feet myself, and then I finally noticed the blue sign with white text above the station exit: Lancaster Gate.

I turned, barely avoiding colliding with someone else, and sprinted down the road.

We both regretted what we were saying even as we said it, but we couldn't seem to stop. And then you paused, your eyes drifting to the carpet as you finally said something else.

"I think . . . I think maybe you should go."

"What?"

You nodded, still not meeting my eyes. "This isn't what either of us want."

Suddenly, all the other words were trapped in my throat. I cleared it, then again, as I tried to find the right ones to convince you to stop. To take it back. But you just stood there in silence, staring at the floor.

I'd never been a runner, or an athlete of any type—you'd

tried convincing me to go to the gym with you, once, but after I'd whined and complained the entire time, I think you decided to cut your losses.

Now, I sprinted through the streets, ignoring the pain on my side and in my back, the burn in my chest, the taste of iron in the back of my mouth. All around me, others did the same, shoving their way between people and narrowly dancing out of the way of cars that tore down the road. As I turned the corner, I noticed one of the city's double-decker buses idling in the middle of the road. Its doors were held open, and no one was inside.

I was navigating the streets by memory, not even slowing to second-guess myself. I couldn't have afforded to anyway, but this wasn't a choice I made consciously. My jacket flapped behind me as I ran. Its plastic-y fabric snapping, along with my ragged breathing, was the only sound I heard.

It was the fastest I'd ever run, the fastest I'd ever followed this route. But the twenty-minute trip that had taken me fifteen was the longest of my life. At one point, I slammed hard against the metal frame of one of the city's telephone boxes, pain shooting up my already bloodied palms. The phone inside dangled uselessly from the hook, its cord still swaying. I pushed off of the box and continued down the road. And as I finally neared the building, looking up at your window, the sky above was starting to darken, a shadow moving over the earth.

Later that night, I stood still, watching your shadow pace back and forth in front of the window. Every few steps, your arm moved up to your face—wiping away tears. Out here, my own face and neck burned, even in the cool, calm air. My throat closed in on itself, around all the words I wished I'd said to you instead.

But this time was different. I knew it was too late.

So eventually, I sucked in a breath, the air sharp against my lungs. I held it for a moment, then let it go. And then I turned and let you go, too.

I didn't slow as I reached the building, just ran into the wall as I began hammering the doorbell. The blood rushing past my ears and my heartbeat thudding in my chest nearly drowned out the noise as it unlocked, but then the door swung open, and I tumbled up the steps to your flat. I pounded on your door, nearly collapsing when it swung open in front of me.

And then you were standing there. Your eyes met mine, swirling with so many emotions, and I was sure mine reflected the same back at you. I opened my mouth, and the ghost of your name prickled in my throat, stinging up into my eyes and making it hard to swallow.

You turned away, back into your living room, the door still ajar. I followed you in, frowning, until I saw you gathering your things into a bag. I peeked at it as you disappeared into your bedroom—at the belongings you were trying to save. And then I understood.

These weren't essentials. They were memories: the blanket your grandmother knitted you as a child, the good luck charm you'd kept on the corner of your desk, a book of the letters your parents had sent you in the year after you moved out to live on your own. And at the top of the pile was a framed photo. Of us.

Finally, I found my voice. I said your name, and I heard your shuffling from the other room stop. A moment later, you stood in the doorway, looking into the living room at me. You were crying again, only this time, you moved toward me, collapsing against my chest. I held you close, as tightly as I could, as if I could mold your body to mine. And suddenly I was crying too.

We're too late to run—we both know it. I don't know if it would make a difference if we did. The shadow outside has grown larger, darkening the sky like that eclipse we watched together so many years ago, paper glasses pressed to our eyes.

I don't know how long we stay like this, either, but time no longer exists for me. As the end of the world catapults toward us, suddenly all the words we left unsaid that night don't need to be said anymore. I simply hold you, for seconds or maybe hours, breathing in your scent, feeling your heart thumping in time with mine. Nothing matters anymore except you.

In the moments before it stops, everything is right with the world.

Artificial

T HE AIR IN HERE was musty. Stale. There wasn't a
speck of dust in sight, yet the smell of it permeated
the air—enough that I twitched my nose, warding off a
sneeze. I paused for a moment, waiting as the sensation
built up in my chest and my face twisted into a grimace
in anticipation.

The sneeze never came.

I sighed, scratched at the stubble on my chin, and kept
walking.

I made my way to the wall on the left, coming upon
my first painting of the day. The gilt frame around it
stretched just out of my reach in every direction, showing
its age in the tarnish and dirt worn into the intricate
grooves. I had to squat to read the neat print on the small
white placard underneath it. *Helping Hands.* I took a step
back to admire the canvas.

Calling it a canvas might've been a misnomer. "Painting" probably was, too, for that matter. The space for

the physical artwork had long ago been replaced with a high-definition screen, its colors just slightly too vivid under the room's bright lights. Between the screen's glow and the fluorescent bulbs, there was no need for the gallery lights that still hung above the frame. But my attention had years ago moved beyond the color of the screen, and the picture lights that had been switched off, and the antique frame that surrounded it.

Today, I focused on the strange amalgamation of too-smooth shapes and skin tones melding together in the image in front of me. At a glance, it sort of looked like people clasping hands, arms reaching from one edge of the frame to grasp those on the other side. But their fingers seemed to form together or lengthen as they outstretched. A child's hand became that of an adult where another arm crossed in front of it. Lines within the image blurred into nothing and came from nowhere, and smaller details—fingernails, the bones and knuckles beneath the skin, the freckles and veins and the wrinkles in people's palms—were missing or just . . . wrong. The more I stared, the more I noticed, and the less like hands they looked at all.

I moved to the next painting.

The second display was in a similar frame as the first, with a card that read *The Secret Garden*. A green expanse reached toward the sky from behind an iron trellis, vines and leaves weaving through one another. Colorful blooms peeked out from between the stems in all different shapes and shades. Then I spotted one collection of blush-colored petals that grew from the dinner-plate-sized leaf of a tropical plant. A tangle of ivy encircled the plants and the trellis, until it turned into one of the iron bars itself. It was hard to tell where one plant started and another began, and as I studied the screen, I started to wonder whether it wasn't all somehow the *same* plant, with the way the stems and greenery seemed to sprout from one shadow in the lower corner.

It took about an hour to work my way through the rest of the gallery and its displays—an otherworldly neon cityscape, a busy park, swirls of deep blues and greens that might've been an ocean or an aurora in a starless night sky. The pieces each were pretty enough from a distance, but they all turned strange the longer I looked. But that was art, wasn't it? It was true for all of it I'd ever seen, at least. I'd come here every day for as long as I could remember, wandering through the gallery, hearing every cough and every footstep I made echo off the displays until I had observed each piece.

The cold, unnatural light of the museum made way for the warm afternoon sun as I stepped out onto the sidewalk. I squinted, my eyes adjusting as I made my way down the street to the grocery store. As I walked,

I shrugged my shoulders against the wind; even with the warmth of the sun on my skin, goosebumps still prickled along my arms as I walked.

It was a short trek, though the museum was technically in the opposite direction of the path I would've traced from my house. It would've been easier to avoid the diversion altogether and spend the extra time watching something on TV or scrolling the internet. The truth was that there was an ache I felt somewhere deep in my chest, a longing I couldn't explain that drew me back to the paintings time and again. Every day I woke up, sat down at my computer to work, visited the museum, bought groceries, ate, slept. Tedium after tedium, and repeat. I knew the algorithms would match me with someone when the time was right; that was why they existed, after all—to remove the guesswork and messiness. Until then, though, the gallery's unsettling artwork felt like the only chance for something new to come into my life, for something to change.

But nothing ever did, except for the paintings on the walls.

The next day, the placards and paintings were all new. *Dinner Party* was an expanse of food across a long table, every square inch covered in bowls of fruit, roasted birds, and toothache-inducing desserts. The fruit wasn't anything I recognized, and the desserts were arranged in impossible configurations, but it was at least fun to imagine the extravagance. *Storm in the Canyon* showed a massive cloud stretching over the desert, with lightning spidering in every direction—even upward, ending somewhere beyond the top of the frame.

I smiled a little as I reached the back wall, where three smaller frames created a series of images. Each showed a forest animal playing a different instrument: a fox with a clarinet, a bear with a trombone, an owl with a flute. The animals looked uncomfortably realistic, and their paws (or wing, in the owl's case) contorted into something almost human in order to fit the instruments. Music staffs also traced along the bottom of each frame, though the notes themselves didn't match any symbols I had ever seen. Of course, I was no true aficionado; I had never managed to get past the discordant notes and halting melodies of the songs that streamed on the radio. After a few more minutes, I walked to the next screen, absentmindedly humming a tune under my breath that I imagined would've fit the woodland trio better.

Then, out of the corner of my eye, something moved. I paused, and my humming stopped. I turned around, surveying the rest of the museum. My eyes scanned the whitewashed walls of the room, but I was the only one here. I was always the only one anywhere. I turned back to the frame in front of me, then caught it again. A flicker.

I frowned, leaning forward until I could make out the pixels in the screen. You weren't supposed to touch the artwork, but . . .

A few seconds passed while I stared at the piece, but nothing else happened. Eventually, I grew bored. I took a step back to take in the next painting as usual, and by the time I left to go find food, the moment had slipped my mind entirely.

As soon as I stepped foot in the museum the next day, something seemed . . . different. The air didn't feel quite as stuffy, and it seemed almost cooler than usual. I contemplated the sensations only briefly before shrugging them off. It had been a frustrating day at work, dealing with far too many numbers and figures; maybe I was just eager for the change of pace.

As I moved through the exhibit, however, my feelings of unease grew. The gallery was truly just one large room, with partial walls in the middle that added space for more frames to be displayed. If anything had been drastically different, I would've spotted it as I walked in. Yet . . .

It wasn't until I reached the back wall that my unease turned to true confusion. Back here, the smell of stale air was gone entirely, and the slight tang of mildew tickled my nose in its place. I didn't even pay attention to the new images as I tried to find the source of the smell. Then I spotted it. In the far left corner, behind a partition that kept it out of view from the front of the gallery, a utility door hung just slightly ajar. In all the years I'd spent walking through this space, I couldn't even remember if I'd noticed it before—but now my eyes trained on the soft yellow glow that seemed to come from behind it.

After a moment's hesitation, I abandoned the day's paintings and headed toward the door.

The creak as the old hinges saw use again was quieter than I'd expected, but it still echoed through the room as I stepped inside. Beneath my feet, the ground went from solid concrete to gritty hardwood; the layers of dirt and grime softened my footfalls. The room looked like an extension of the gallery, if the museum had been transported twenty years into the future. *Or if the museum had been abandoned twenty years in the past*, I thought as I took in the sight before me.

In the dirt that had collected on the floor, a few weeds and blades of grass had somehow found a home and managed to grow in the dark. Gone were the pristine white walls and the artificial buzz of ceiling lights in the main wing of the museum. Here, the only glow came from the portrait light on the wall directly ahead of me, framed by two matching staircases that climbed into the ceiling, to a second floor I hadn't realized existed. The rest of the room disappeared into shadows in either direction.

But none of that drew my attention once I spotted the simple gold frame in front of me, and the image inside it. I stepped forward, sneezing as my shoes kicked the scent of damp earth into the air. This piece of art was not like any I'd seen before. To start, this was a true canvas, not a bright, high-resolution screen. I could see individual brushstrokes crisscrossing the stretched cloth. And the painting itself . . . I had to remind myself to breathe as my eyes soaked in the details. Hands reached toward each other from opposite corners of the frame, caught in a freeze frame seconds away from brushing fingertips, forever out of each other's reach. The delicate fingers, the light and shadows dancing across their palms, the muscles and tendons in their wrists were all somehow captured perfectly.

For a time, I forgot I was standing there.

I could understand the love and longing between them, could somehow feel the gentle touch that hadn't even happened yet between the hands in the artwork—a touch that I'd forgotten myself. Absentmindedly, I brushed my fingertips against each other, mirroring the hands in the painting. As I stared at it, I could almost will myself to believe the tickle of warmth against my skin wasn't my own . . .

It was only as I felt the air around me growing cooler that I thought to look at my watch. My heart leapt as I read the time. I headed toward the secret door, taking one last look back at the painting as I crossed the threshold into the main gallery. I eased the door shut behind me, then slipped out of the museum and back out onto the sidewalk under the glow of the streetlamps.

I tossed and turned that night as I tried to sleep, and I could barely focus on work the next day. The sandwich I'd made for lunch grew cold and soggy on the plate beside me. I'd cobbled it together from leftovers I'd had in the fridge, but I'd been lucky I'd even had food left over—with my groceries pre-selected each day based on previous shopping history, dietary restrictions, and my average consumption rate, it was rare for me to have much in my fridge beyond what the store had predicted I'd eat.

Even if I had received my usual allotment of food the day before, though, it wouldn't have mattered. With only a few halfhearted nibbles taken from one corner, I practically skipped eating altogether. In every quiet moment, my mind drifted back to the museum, to that painting. The hands on the clock moved as if they were ticking through molasses, constantly reaching for each other, then being forced apart. And then, finally, the workday ended. Without wasting a second more, I closed my laptop and raced out the door to the museum.

As I stepped through the doors to the main gallery, I skipped the pretense of looking at the artwork on the walls; I headed straight for the door in the far left corner.

It was locked.

I jiggled the handle, even gave it a slight shove with my shoulder, thinking back to how it had creaked when I'd swung it open yesterday. Maybe age and disuse had warped the wood of the doorframe or rusted the hinges to make them stick. But it still didn't budge.

I sighed, glancing behind me at the glow from the other frames. Before yesterday, I would've happily taken the time to look at each one, to stand back and try to make sense of the strange scenes and unfamiliar creatures they depicted. Now, the vivid colors and shapes they threw out from the sterile walls might as well have been in grayscale. I glanced halfheartedly at a few of them, that empty ache in my chest somehow better and worse at having been in that room, having taken in a painting that was both duller and more alive than anything on those screens.

As I made my way to the grocery store, I chewed on the strangeness of the past two days—first the mystery wing opening up, then it being locked away again. Something had opened up within me too, but I couldn't lock it away, couldn't conceal it behind a door or go on the way I had before. I'd been missing something in my life, something from the artwork I'd always admired; it had needled my brain for as long as I could remember, an errant detail I'd dismissed until I'd seen that hidden gallery and the small painting hanging on the wall. Now, the flaw in the forgery was clear, and all I wanted was to see the real thing.

I forced myself to go through the rest of my evening routine as normal: I went to the grocery store to pick up my meals, went home to prepare them, went to bed when the lights in my apartment dimmed automatically. But I didn't change clothes, only lay on my back on top of the sheets. I counted the seconds as they ticked by, and I sat up once I reached nine thousand.

Exactly midnight.

I moved off the mattress, headed downstairs, and slipped out the door.

I started down the same path I always had, but as I walked, I couldn't help but marvel at how different the world felt at night. Stars sparkled in the wide expanse of sky, dimming to almost nothing underneath the streetlamps. A cool breeze ruffled my hair and underneath the fabric of my unzipped jacket—not in a way that sent me shivering or shying away, though. I welcomed it, breathing deeply. Each step forward felt lighter, and the ache in my chest eased as I drew closer.

None of this was actually breaking any rules—at least not spoken ones. I had always had the freedom to go wherever I'd like, to make my own choices and live my life as I saw fit. Nothing beyond my job forced me into a routine, and even that could change if I really wanted. But it was always easier to listen to the recommendations, to follow the suggestions offered all around me. Take this moment, for instance. I'd stayed awake after my apartment had suggested I go to sleep, gone for a walk when the world was dark, and now ended up at the museum for the second time that day.

But the door to the inside was locked.

The lightness in my step was replaced with a lead weight in my stomach. Peering through the glass doors, my breath fogging the glass, I could see the gallery inside was dark, the frames all empty screens, waiting for the next day's artwork and for the world to wake up to view them. Of course they were. Why would any of it need to exist when I wasn't meant to be awake? The longer I stood here, the more the realization I'd had as I'd eaten dinner—that the maintenance door inside must unlock somehow, so maybe I'd be able to sneak in and play with the latch until it opened—made my cheeks burn even in the dark. It all just seemed foolish now.

The cool air from before had a bite to it once more as I crossed the street to head back to my apartment, and I felt my eyelids droop at the late hour. This had all been a mistake, one I knew I would pay for tomorrow. I should've listened to the suggestions, trusted the automations that were there to make my life easier rather than complicating—

A rustle of fabric behind me stopped my thoughts, and me, in my tracks. I turned around and squinted through the night, scanning the building's facade. Was it my ears or my eyes playing tricks on me? Nothing had changed with the door, but where I'd been a moment before, I saw a strange shadow. The shadow moved just slightly, catching the edge of the light beam from the lamp nearby. In that moment, it turned into a figure, the light making her features seem harsher and somehow even more alive as she stood unmoving, watching me as I watched her. Time stopped; her dark hair was the only thing that stirred as a breeze cut through the air between us. Something prickled on the back of my neck, a warmth deep inside, like I'd felt in the abandoned gallery.

Then she moved, stepping toward me, and time started again, and I spun back around before her foot hit the pavement, my heart hammering in my chest as I ran.

My heart was still racing when I woke up the next morning. Maybe that was a misnomer; "waking up" would imply I slept. Crawling back into bed after I'd returned to my apartment, I'd tossed and turned the rest of the night until I was tangled in my sheets. And when sunlight began to filter through the blinds and lightened the room, I'd rolled over and found myself staring at my alarm clock, once again counting the seconds, until a sharp tone finally pierced through the quiet, telling me to get up.

As I moved through the start of my day, getting myself ready and then sitting down in front of my computer for work, I realized how similar it all felt to the day before. But I felt different. Part of me wished I could pretend the night before had been a dream, and that this routine was what I wanted. It *was* what I wanted. I wanted to go back to how things had been before, when my days were made up of work and the ever-changing museum pieces—from the main gallery, not a hidden one in a back room—and the grocery store and sleep.

There was nothing wrong in what I'd done . . . at least, I didn't think there was. But I'd never once been out so late, and I couldn't remember the last time I'd seen someone, anyone—much less anyone like the woman who'd been staring at me from the museum entrance as I'd crossed the street. All through the day, as I combed through spreadsheets and tried to find a glimpse of the order and routine I was used to, the panicked race of my heartbeat never seemed to slow, and my hands twisted together in my lap. When I rose from my seat at the end of the day and gathered my jacket to walk down the road, I tried to push the memories of the same walk the night before from my mind. Everything was normal, back to what it had been before. The more I thought about it, felt the anxiety crushing against my chest and the nights of sleeplessness weighing on my eyelids, the more I started to wonder . . .

Maybe there was a reason that painting had been locked behind a door all this time.

With each step that brought me closer to the museum, I breathed in deeper, pushing thoughts of the abandoned gallery away with each exhale. Of course, I wanted to see it again, but maybe it was for the best that I return to what I knew, to the paintings that left my mind as quickly as they appeared on the walls each morning and the routine that had filled my days for as long as I could remember. By the time I reached the glass doors of the gallery, I was almost smiling at the thought of it. I reached out, grasped the cold metal of the door handle in my palm, and pulled.

It didn't move.

I tried again. Nothing. The panic in my chest returned, this time with another feeling that sat in my stomach like acid, that burned in my cheeks and stung behind my eyes. I threw my weight against the door, nearly losing my balance, but the door stayed stubbornly still.

I glanced around behind me, suddenly on edge for another reason. The museum had never been closed before, for as long as I'd visited here. I had only encountered it locked the night before—right before I'd seen the woman.

I squinted into the sunlight, panning over the scene for anything, or anyone, out of place. Unease crawled up my neck as I looked over the road, the streetlight, the trees beside me. But the tree limbs hardly rustled, and my shadow stood alone against the pavement. Only one detail stood out in the scene as I studied it: a small piece of paper lying in the grass a few feet away.

I bent down and picked it up, reading the neat handwriting three times before it seemed to make sense. I glanced back at the locked museum, then at the note once more.

What's it worth to you?

The acid that I'd felt in my stomach rose into my throat.

I couldn't bring myself to continue my walk to the grocery store, and anyway, I doubted I'd be able to eat anything tonight if I tried. Instead, I returned to my apartment, the note caught tight in my fist.

I couldn't decide what it meant, and maybe that was what bothered me so much. Maybe it was that I didn't know who'd written the note, or how to answer them.

And maybe it was that I wasn't sure what my answer should be.

I wasn't sure how long I sat at my dining room table, staring at those five words, but it was long enough for the light outside to dim and the curl of each letter to imprint itself on my eyelids, so even when I closed my eyes, I saw it staring back at me. What was the museum worth to me? I knew what it was starting to cost me, at least. The answer to that was "my sanity."

After a while, when the lights in my apartment dimmed, I convinced myself to put the paper down and head to bed. As much as the worry gnawed at my insides, I could hardly keep my eyes open after two sleepless nights. Maybe if I followed the suggestions, listened to the algorithms, things would go back to normal. Eventually, I'd forget about the painting. I'd get to see the art in the museum again. No, none of it would be the same as what I'd found behind the locked door, but I'd get used to the ache in my chest after a while. I'd looked past the details before; I could learn to do it again.

In fact, by the next morning, I'd decided that must've been what the note meant. It wasn't a threat—just another suggestion, with my best interest in mind. As I sat down with my cobbled-together breakfast, I thought about heading to the grocery store tonight and wondered at what I'd find in my bags when I brought them home. I would try the museum again in a few days, after I'd returned to my routine and proven I'd put the hidden gallery out of my thoughts. Maybe, in the meantime, I could try a more complicated recipe if I had extra time in the evening. I grabbed my grocery list off the counter and brought it to the table with me, picking up the note from the night before and setting it aside. And then I stopped.

There was more to the note.

I wasn't sure how I'd missed it the night before, but the paper was much too thick against my fingertips, and in the morning light, the wrinkles in the note showed that it had been folded in half. I reached for it again and unfolded it with shaky hands . . . and revealed the pencil sketch of another set of hands—ones that had been in my thoughts since I'd first seen them.

What's it worth to you?

I stared at the pencil sketch, tracing each perfect line with my gaze. A series of graphite scratches on paper formed the creases and shadows of each fingernail and knuckle and wrinkle in the skin. One hand reaching pleadingly for the other, the second reaching back. Now, though, I didn't think they were out of each other's reach—maybe they were only seconds away from touching.

It took me a moment to tear my eyes away from the drawing, but as my thumb shifted, another set of words appeared below it at the bottom of the paper scrap: *Time to turn a corner.*

The question on the note had never been about the museum. And as the second message played in my mind, it formed into a decision. This time, I didn't stop and think about it, or wait for the opportune moment. I got up, leaving everything except for the note, and headed toward the door.

As I stepped outside, the cold morning air was sharp against my skin. In just one week, the air had grown crisp and cool, and this early in the morning, I could feel it in my lungs with each breath. I welcomed it, marveling at how it drove the last bit of grogginess from my eyes and quickened my pace along the familiar path.

As I reached the front doors of the museum, I didn't even bother trying the doors to the main gallery to see if they were unlocked; instead, I veered off the pavement and into the grass, heading to the back of the building. As I moved around the corner, behind the trees and shrubs that funneled people toward the front entrance, I felt the ground dip suddenly below my feet; as it did, the grass became longer, wilder, brushing my knees and even the backs of my hands as I walked.

I trudged forward, toward the far corner of the building, where the smooth white limestone had turned gray and dimpled. And then, turning right once more, my heart leapt. I saw what I had been hoping for. A door, just like the one in the museum, heavy metal on old hinges that were rusted from years without use.

It hung ajar.

My heart pounding, I stepped inside, blinking away the dim until I could see clearly after the bright sunlight outside. I was in a dark, empty hallway, but I could feel the soft wood and earth beneath my shoes. In the distance, a faint warm light beckoned me closer. I moved toward it, toward the painting whose sketch I held in my hands.

As I got closer, a shadow moved in my periphery—a figure stood on the stairs near the painting. I stopped, my heart hammering. Then another rose, and a third, her dark hair cascading down her shoulders. She waited a moment, then gestured at me to come forward.

I swallowed, then moved into the light.

"You wrote the note," I said. "You drew the hands." I didn't word it as a question because I already knew the answer.

She nodded.

I nodded too, then looked at the paper still clasped in my hand. I met her eyes once more. "You asked what it's worth?" I took a shaky breath.

She smiled. Her eyes were soft, the same shade of brown as her hair. "You've already answered." She gestured behind her, to the other figures I'd seen on the staircase—a man, his hair a shimmer of silver against his dark skin, and another woman, freckles splashed across her cheekbones and down her arms.

"We all did." It was the man, his voice rich and strong. "Same as you."

Mine warbled by comparison. I couldn't remember ever speaking to another human before. "You all lived out there?"

"We *survived* out there," the other woman said. "But their imitations just imitate themselves now; that's not living."

"You can't automate everything," the man added.

The artist nodded at the man and woman each, then turned to face me. "So . . . are you ready to see the real world?"

She reached a hand toward me, a bit of dried paint

smudged on her fingers. I thought for a moment, then reached my hand out toward hers.

The Choices We Face

WHEN I CLOSE MY eyes, Mom's last warning to me replays itself, down to the tremble in her voice.

"Listen to me: Don't come home."

Regret gnaws at my insides thinking back to it now. I hadn't argued, hadn't put up a fight. I'd done what I was told, even though I was only two hours away.

For once, I shouldn't have listened.

Now they're here, too. And I'm alone.

The staff here at the printing press on the outskirts of town was small—the reporters were supposed to be working from the old newsroom downtown for a couple more months, until the construction was finished on their new offices, so it was just the designers, the IT guy, and me in the warehouse-sized building. Inwardly, I had still been missing my desk tucked away in the corner of the downtown office—I'd traded out the dusty carpet and hum of quiet chatter from the other journalists for the cold cement walls and bangs and clatters of machinery that were impossible to drown out.

Now, of course, I'd had a change of heart. The phones had stopped working long before we'd known what was happening, but the old newsroom was on the busiest street in town. I could only imagine the mess everyone there would've had to face to get away. The closest road that led out of town ran right next to the hospital.

The cement box I'd grumbled about for so long was two and a half miles away, through a mess of trees and winding, hilly back roads that split off toward different factories and manufacturing plants. It was as far from cozy as I could imagine, but it had kept me safe.

For a while, at least.

Another voice plays in my head, this one sending my heart to the pit of my stomach. Just three words: "I love you." But I know how to read every unspoken word that exists between them. Thomas lives states away from here, far from where the outbreak started. But I thought I was far from where it started, too. They made it here within a day; how much farther could they have gone by now?

I glance around at my things. The little bit of food I scrounged from people's desks. My phone, the battery long dead—once my lifeline to my family, to Thomas. Now, it's a relic from an old life. A notebook. My jacket. The first aid kit from bookkeeping.

There's only one thing I'm missing.

I load my supplies into the backpack I took from the office next to mine. It had belonged to the IT guy, Kenneth. I didn't even know him that well, but he'd offered to let me come with his family. He'd helped me when one got in through the window. And when we'd realized it was too late for him, he'd kept me company until . . .

I hesitate at the memory and finish packing.

When I'm done, I slip on my jacket and the backpack, then peer out from the gap in the door. My car is right where I left it, next to Kenneth's truck. There's one of them out there, but if I'm quiet, I should be okay.

With one hand in my jacket pocket, I thumb my car key. I hear Thomas in my head again as I do, this time saying the message I'd heard woven into his other one. *I'll find you.*

I turn and head toward the back wall, by the printing press. This time of day, with the last rays of daylight seeping through the doorway from the windows in the other room, the machinery throws shadows along the floor. A new shadow grows from mine as I take something off the hook on the wall: a crowbar. It's long. Heavy. I noticed it the first day I arrived and never got the chance to ask why it hung there—I guess for moving pallets of newspapers or working the machinery. Now, I'm hoping it's my ticket out of here.

But a ticket to where?

Thomas lives east, too far to predict what I'll find. My family is west, an afternoon's drive, but straight into the heart of the outbreak. And between either place are miles of unknown.

I can get past the one that's out there and make it to my car. But then I have a choice to make. East or west. Thomas or my family.

It's an impossible decision. Except the longer I stand here, watching, the more I realize I've already made it.

I take a steadying breath, tighten my grip on the crow-bar, and open the door.

Part II: What's Left Behind

Silence in the City, pt. 1

M Y FEET SCUFFED AGAINST the pavement as I walked. The sound mixed with the drip of water off the rooftops, beating a steady rhythm that echoed around me. The towering concrete structures on either side of the street amplified all of it: the sound, the solitude, and the silence in between.

You'd think by now I'd have gotten used to it. The quiet. But it had made me uneasy at the start, and it still set my teeth on edge now. No buzzing streetlamps, no idling car engines, no cell phone tones or humming AC units in the windows above. It wasn't any normal power outage, and we'd known it from the start. The stillness that had settled over everything in those initial moments after the blackout had never gone away. Just like the darkness, it smothered everything in the city.

After four and a half months, it was starting to smother us.

Even though the rain had let up an hour ago, the clouds

lingered. They made the usually dim streets this time of day even more difficult to navigate, but at least it gave me something else to focus on. I kept my head tucked and my eyes trained on the sidewalk, trying not to trip as I made my way farther into the city. Somewhere nearby, a coyote yipped. I searched for a moment before I finally spotted him. He stood in the road about half a block away, his ears pricked toward me. He sniffed the air and stared at me for a moment, his eyes wide.

"And what are you doing out here?" I asked aloud. At the sound of my voice, even just barely above a whisper, he turned and sprinted in the other direction. Evidently, his answer was the same as mine. I sighed, then continued on.

I could tell when I neared the center of the city. The first sign was the stench. No one had ever considered how bad the apocalypse would smell, I'd come to realize. Maybe calling this an apocalypse seemed dramatic, but after four months without lawn mowers or garbage trucks, it certainly looked the way movies had always shown it. Trash spilled out from the dumpsters and covered the ground, piling like snowbanks against the sides of buildings. Weeds sprouted up between cracks in the asphalt that had gone unfilled and mostly untrodden. I wrinkled my nose and veered toward the street instead, beginning to weave around and climb over the abandoned cars that blocked my path. Once, they had probably been in some version of organized lanes. But now a lot of their windows had been smashed, their contents raided. Glass crunched underfoot with almost every step I took. Many of the cars had been pushed against each other too, forming a makeshift barrier with few paths left to get through it.

That was the second sign.

I forced myself to take my time moving past the barrier, trying to ignore the sense of dread that was starting to press against the inside of my chest. Taking deep, even breaths, I slid across the hood of a cab and crawled onto the next. After another couple of cars, I reached a delivery truck. This one was much too tall to climb over, and I paused, unsure of where to go from here. The passenger window was one of the few still intact. *Of course it would be,* I thought. But a quick glance down the row told me getting through wasn't going to be easier anywhere else; this must've been the spot. I chewed my lower lip and looked back at the truck in front of me. The gap between the car I crouched on now and the door was maybe wide enough . . .

I reached up to the door handle and closed my eyes in a quick prayer. I pulled the handle and felt a click. Unlocked. I let out a soft breath and opened the door a bit wider, just enough for me to squeeze into the cab and crawl through. I opened the other door on the driver's side and hopped down to the ground, keeping my head low and pressing myself against the side of the truck.

My hunch had been right. The difference on this side of the pileup was stark—the street was clear for almost a block, and from what I could see, the cars and trucks that had been pushed out of the way made an almost impassable barrier the entire way around. By now, the sun had almost set, and though my eyes were adjusted to the dimness, it still took me a moment to get my bearings. Finally, I spotted a handful of faint, warm lights in some of the windows farther down the row, and a figure moved near one of them. A second later, the light snuffed out, and the window disappeared into the shadows surrounding it.

I stayed crouched and pressed against the row of cars as I moved in the direction of the candlelight, keeping my head on a swivel for the slightest sound or shuffle of movement in my periphery. These days, it wasn't odd that people were already dousing their candles and turning in for the night, even though it was just a few minutes past twilight. Better not to be noticed—you stayed safer that way.

The end of the row of cars jutted up against an iron gate at the entrance to an alleyway. The gate was padlocked shut, but looking at it up close, I doubted it would be much of an issue to climb. I waited for a beat and surveyed my surroundings a final time. Still no one. But I needed to be fast. You couldn't trust the people out after dark anymore. They weren't kind or forgiving, and they wouldn't wait for your explanation. They were desperate or dangerous—oftentimes both.

And tonight, I was one of them.

I slid my empty backpack off my shoulders and swung it over the gate, watching as it disappeared into the shadows on the other side. Then, I took hold of the iron bars and heaved myself upward.

Past the gate, no one had bothered locking the doors to the building. It took more effort just to find the handle in the low light than it did to get inside. Once I did, I eased it closed behind me as quickly as I could, keeping the handle turned until I was sure it wouldn't click shut.

In here, I was amazed to realize I could actually see. The door had opened into a long hallway, lined along either side with candles spaced a few feet apart on the floor. They were obviously scavenged—there was a hodgepodge of decoratively carved wax sculptures and tea lights, plain outdoor candles that created puddles of wax and scented monstrosities that chased away any lingering odors from the garbage outside. A menorah even burned in one corner, a few of its candles missing from their holders. Their flames all wavered in the breeze that had snuck in behind me, casting hazy shadows on the walls, and whether from their glow or the solid structure around me, I almost felt warm. I adjusted the backpack straps on my shoulders and started to make my way down the hallway.

In a past life, I'd known this building. At the very least, I'd known what it housed: a homeless shelter on the first floor, always with more mouths to feed than food in their pantry, with three floors of tired-looking apartments above that. I'd only been inside once, briefly, to ask directions when I'd first moved here. But I'd walked past it almost every day on my way to work, always waving to the kind man who ran the place. He was older, with soft, wise eyes that left the joy and heartache the city brought him tattooed on his face. I wondered if his eyes told a different story now.

As I walked farther, I decided it wouldn't have mattered if I'd been in the building a thousand times. This was as if I'd entered into a maze, and the mismatched scents in the air just added to the confusion. The only sense of direction I had were the rows of candles that illuminated some paths and left others cloaked in darkness. Around every new corner, my heart halted with my breath, just waiting for me to make one wrong turn. One noise. One mistake. It didn't help that I only had a hunch as to where I was headed. But I didn't have a choice in any of this. I needed what was in that stockpile.

Rounding another corner, my demeanor changed. This was something different: an entryway at the end of the hall, with a faint light filtering from inside. I forced myself to move forward slowly, padding along at the same speed as before. I kept my eyes trained on the glow that bounced off the back wall of the open room. No shadow. No flicker of movement. I was only a couple feet away now. For another brief moment, I hesitated, pressing my back against the wall nearby. I listened.

As always, there was only silence.

I exhaled, then turned back to the entryway and stepped inside. But the sight made me pause in my tracks. In all my time spent thinking about this room, this wasn't what I'd imagined. It was so much better. Every surface was hidden under rows of canned food, and bags of rice and flour piled atop one another in the far corner. On the wall to my right, a message had been scrawled in paint across a large metal door: DO NOT OPEN. It was the door to an industrial-sized walk-in freezer. I turned around and admired it all, for a few seconds forgetting my urgency. But a creaking floor somewhere above me broke my trance. I slid my backpack off my shoulders and got to work.

I kept a steady, methodical clip as I moved about the kitchen, barely stopping as I grabbed each new item and added it to my pack. There was *so much* here. I repeated my list over and over in my head as I went, not so much worried I'd forget something as I was worried I'd weigh myself down with things I didn't need. The cans were first—they were heaviest and took up the most space. I couldn't make out their labels in the dim light, but I grabbed the largest I could find and hoped they were worth taking. As I moved closer to the back wall, I noticed some boxes of pasta and took those too, stuffing them in beside the cans. I could only fit one bag of rice on top of everything else, but it would have to do. Finally, I turned and headed back toward the freezer.

Just before I reached the metal door, I set my backpack down gently on the floor beside me. The last thing I needed was the bag hitting one of the metal shelves inside or knocking something over. I picked up the one candle in the room and brought its glow over to the door. Just as I'd done with the outside door, I turned the handle all the way and eased this one open, wincing a little as the rubber seal on the inside released. But the sound had been barely audible even to me, so I stepped through the doorway and began searching the shelves.

Amazingly, it was still chilly in here. The shelves

weren't quite as full as the counters outside, but this was still more food than I'd seen in a long time. My stomach growled at the thought of it. But it wasn't what I was after. I moved farther back and continued looking.

The items I'd come for were on the farthest shelf. It was the flash of orange that caught my eye in the candlelight, and my heart leapt. Prescription bottles were piled into labeled trays or set in neat rows beside them, labels all facing outward. I found the ones I was looking for and slipped as many of the vials as I could into my pocket. As I moved the last one out of the way, something glinted at me from the back of the shelf. I frowned. The candle's glow wasn't bright enough for me to make out quite what it was. I reached my arm back and felt around, palming a small round package. My eyes widened. Batteries. I fit my hand around a few and pulled them out into the open.

"Don't move."

The voice sent ice through my veins. I did as I was told.

I heard the girl's footsteps behind me as she moved closer. "Put your hands up, and turn around. Slowly."

I swallowed the lump forming in my throat. I used my fingertips to slide the small battery packages up my sleeve, then raised my hands and shuffled around to face her. It was hard to tell in the candlelight, but she looked just a little younger than me. Her eyes flashed with danger and fear, as if she were the animal who had been cornered instead of me. My eyes drifted downward to the knife that quivered in her hand.

"Please," I tried, pulling my attention away from the knife and back to her. My voice trembled a little. "Please, you don't understand."

She stepped forward, closing the distance between us. The point of her knife was inches away from my chest. I tried to move away, but my back was already pressed against the shelving.

"Stop talking." She spoke softly, but her tone sliced the air. I began to sweat, and my gaze flashed toward the exit.

This time, I felt the point of the knife press against my chest. "Don't even think about it," the girl warned. I looked back at her. She studied me for a moment, then glanced at my hand. "Give me the candle."

I hesitated. I could feel the bottles I'd stashed in my pocket against my side, the packages of batteries in my sleeve scratching against my arm. I was so close.

After a few seconds, I held out the candle. She reached her hand out to take it, relief playing across her face. Just as her fingertips brushed mine, I tipped it to the side.

The girl cried out and leapt backward as melted wax dripped down her fingers. I darted past her and lunged blindly for the exit. The wax had extinguished the candle's flame, plunging the room into black once more, but I could just make out an outline of the doorway—

My foot caught on one of the shelves, and I stumbled, landing hard on my knee. As I tried to stand, I felt a whisper of motion beside me and swung my arm out, connecting with something. Immediately, a white heat radiated down my fingertips, and I sucked in a breath. The girl's knife clattered against the floor. I heard her scramble for it, so I did the same, patting around until my hand hit against something metal. I picked it up and held it in front of me as I tried to stand. Suddenly, she slammed into me. I fell backward, hitting my head against one of the shelves.

I blinked a couple of times, seeing stars even in the pitch black. My hand felt wet and sticky. The knife was gone. I looked down toward my feet, and I heard a small whimper.

My breath hitched in my throat. For a moment, I forgot how to make myself move. I took a step and tripped over the girl's outstretched arm, slamming my knee against the ground again as I fell. I swallowed, then picked myself up and ran my hand along one of the shelves until I found the door.

Back in the kitchen, the light from the hallway filtered in enough for me to make out the shape of my backpack in the corner. I slid it onto my back, then looked back at the freezer door, still hanging ajar. Somewhere above me, voices murmured to each other, and footfalls thudded against the floor. Panic filled my chest. I limped over to the metal door and swung it closed.

Then, I ran.

⸻

By the time I reached the outskirts of the city, the sky was starting to lighten. My lungs burned, and my knee throbbed. I didn't dare slow down though, not until I saw the house with the crumbling front porch. The buckets for collecting rainwater were still outside from the day before. Exhausted, I pulled myself up the front steps and unlocked the door.

Just as I'd expected, she was sitting at the dining table, waiting for me.

"Oh," she breathed, hurrying over. "You're back. I was so worried. It was taking so long, and the . . ." She fell silent, reaching out and hugging me. I tried to return the gesture, but my arms were made of lead. "Did you find it?"

I forced a small smile, then slipped my backpack off my shoulders. She took it from me and unzipped it, setting it down on the floor to get a better look. Her eyes widened at the food, and she covered her mouth with her hand.

"Thank you," she said. "This is . . . this is perfect."

"I found this too," I said. Somehow, my voice didn't

shake, even as I felt like I sucked in each ragged breath from underwater. I pulled my arm out of the sleeve of my jacket, letting the batteries fall to the ground. Then, I fished one of the vials out of my pocket and held it out. She took both in her hands, for a moment just looking at them. Tears welled in her eyes.

"Is she back yet?" A tiny voice came from around the corner, still sounding thick with sleep. A moment later, the brown-haired boy it belonged to found his way over to his older sister. He rubbed his eyes with one hand, maintaining a fierce grip on his stuffed dog with the other.

"She just got back. Look what she brought you, Jamie. She got us food and more of your medicine." She knelt down to his level, pointing at the backpack and then showing him the vial. He studied everything for a moment, then smiled.

"I'm sorry I couldn't grab more," I said. "I tried, but—"

"No, no, this is more than enough. You—" Her voice cracked. "You've saved his life."

My mouth felt dry. I tried to smile, but I couldn't manage it. I nodded instead, looking down at my feet.

"Are you okay?" Jamie's voice made me look up. He furrowed his brow and pointed at me with his free hand. "You're bleeding."

I held my arm up and noticed the deep red stain on my

sleeve for the first time. I took a shaky breath. "I'm . . . It's not my—"

"It looks like you sliced it on something," his sister interrupted. "Let me see it." She took my arm daintily in her hands, her fingertips brushing along the edge of my ripped sleeve. "Well, I don't think it'll need stitches, but let's clean it up and see. I'll go get my first aid kit. There's some water in the bathroom, if you want to go wash." She looked at me, her forehead wrinkled in concern, and placed a hand on my shoulder. There was more she wanted to say, I could tell. More she wanted to ask. But she would wait until Jamie was asleep. I nodded and headed down the hall.

As I watched the dirty water swirl down the drain, I realized I wasn't sure how much of the blood I'd cleaned off my arm was truly mine. It had been so dark, and my brain was still fuzzy . . .

Her words replayed on a loop in my mind. *You've saved his life.* But was this how I was supposed to feel? Another sound was invading my head too, at times far louder than anything else—that girl's whimper as she lay on the floor of the freezer. I squeezed my eyes shut and braced against the side of the sink, willing the noise to stop.

I had to remember why I did this. Who I did it for. I looked up again and studied my reflection in the mirror. I thought back to the man who'd worked at the shelter before the blackout. I thought about his eyes. Looking at my reflection now, mine told a story all their own. They were the same as the coyote's from the day before—dark and wild, darting around as much as my thoughts. I was just as much a frightened animal as the girl in the freezer had been. But there was something else in my eyes too, the more I looked at them. I hadn't seen it in her eyes, but I saw it in mine. Determination.

I'd done what I needed to do to protect the people I loved. That was all that mattered.

I took a deep breath, then another.

Slowly, the sounds in my mind stopped, and there was silence once again.

What's Left Behind

NOTHING SURPRISES ME ANYMORE, yet the feeling I get as the dilapidated wooden fence comes into view causes a small hitch in my breath. As I pick my way through the gray brambles and overgrown shrubs to unlatch the gate, there is a painful longing in my chest, an echo of old memories that I thought I left behind long ago.

The latch is rusted through; I can open it without effort. But as I step through the gate, I can tell it wasn't time that first broke it. The house in front of me is at once exactly as I remembered and unrecognizable—I could've drawn the three large windows, the arch of the roof, and the stairs up to the patio that wrapped around to the back door by memory, but the house I knew didn't have the shattered glass lining the patio or the ivy climbing along the walls and through the crevices that have formed after so many years of neglect. It didn't have the large hole gaping in the roof, exposing rafters and beams—and what is left of that side of the house—to the elements.

My feet rustle in the crisped grass, kicking up the dust that coats the ground like dandelion fluff. It is the only sound other than the wind occasionally knocking the gate and ringing a wind chime somewhere in the distance. There are no other footsteps; my friend is giving me space, which I appreciate. The quiet *shush, shush* of the plants gives way to the crunch of glass, then squeaking hinges as I ease the door open and step inside.

This side of the house is still mostly intact, but it tells a story of what's happened here since I left. The furniture is overturned, and the frames that once hung on the wall have fallen to the ground in piles of glass and wood. Cabinet doors hang ajar, and the shelves inside are picked clean.

The story is a simple one—one that I've written several times over on my own since leaving the caves. Other survivors needed what was here.

I pick my way through other parts of the house. As I go,

I find more of the same in other rooms. In the bathroom, the mirror is hazy with grime, and the medicine cabinet contains only a single bottle of painkillers—empty—lying on its side. In the kitchen, someone has left a pile of used rags in the corner, though maybe this was just an animal trying to find shelter. Water in the sink has sat stagnant for too long and turned murky, and I wrinkle my nose at its smell when I get too close.

I can't fault anyone, human or animal, for trying to make a home out of what is left of mine. That parts of it are even still standing feels surreal. In Missouri, we are far from where the eruption took place, but that just meant we had more time to find shelter. Many of us found refuge in caves; we got to know the world that had existed just underneath our feet while the one we'd known before was wiped clean.

And when we emerged, ash still fell like snow from the sky.

Getting closer to the other end of the house, the ground beneath my feet shifts. Slowly, the hardwood turns to a carpet of dust and dirt and debris, and then my feet begin to leave footprints in blankets of gray. Each step pushes the smell of sulfur into my nose, until I can almost taste the acid of it on the back of my tongue. Then, at the end of the hall, the sky opens up into a harsh light, and the ground in front of me is littered with mounds of what was once the roof.

Rationally, I know I should just turn back. I can imagine the rest of what I will see here, and I know it will still hurt to have my predictions proven true. But I climb anyway, stepping carefully so I don't slip on loose shingles and piles of ash. As I go, using my hands to balance myself on the unsteady footing, I mentally retrace what was here before. *This was Dad's office. This was the living room. That corner was where we put our Christmas tree.*

Someone in the caves tried explaining once what was happening on the surface. They'd found an old history textbook and a map in the front cover, and they traced circles on it that rippled outward. Scientists had known for decades that this would happen one day, what it would cause. Still, though, I imagined them now, picking through the rocks and rubble, seeing entire mountains and cities that have been erased. No amount of planning or understanding could've prepared any of us for this world. We all share a collective shock, and we all need help that no one is able to offer. So we've scavenged and looted what we could find—clothes and blankets, medicine, canned food. Some have done worse. We've all been surviving; returning to normal life feels like forgetting what happened, and most of us aren't ready to do that yet.

I stop, bracing my feet on a splintered beam of wood.

There's a hint of pale paint on the far wall, and a scrap of fabric that I recognize as a tattered bedspread. I look down at my feet, trace through my memory of the space. Yes, I think this is where the bed would've been. In that corner over there, crushed under the weight of the ash and the ceiling, was my dresser.

My gaze spins slowly around the room, rewriting the mental image I had concocted of it as I'd traveled here. Each night, I'd tried to decide what would be left of it, sketching a new idea each time. One version had been blackened and charred by a fire. Another was reclaimed by nature, with plants growing through the floor and climbing vines trailing through the window in search of a refuge from the outside world. Yet another was perfectly intact, with just a layer of dust coating the objects that I'd abandoned here years ago. This is like none of those, and yet it's like all of them.

And then I spot a flash of bright pastel in the corner. I frown and ease myself down from my perch, until the object is within reach. I pick it out of the dust and brush it off. It is a music box—one I'd had in my room since childhood. Somehow, it looks as colorful as I remembered it. I turn it over and twist the key, then open the lid.

A tinkling melody fills the room, and I almost startle at the sound. I hadn't really expected it to work, but the tiny ballerina in the box is spinning around, just as she did before, dancing in front of a tiny mirror and atop a plastic stage. I watch and listen for a moment, entranced by this piece of my old life. The entire world has been paved over, yet this children's toy, of all things, is completely unchanged.

And suddenly it is more than just the smell in the air leaving a sour taste in my mouth. In the tiny mirror, I catch sight of myself—just my eye, staring back at me. But it is a stranger's eye, not the same one that used to reflect back at me from this mirror. This one has seen so much more.

As I stare, the music starts to slow, the rhythm faltering. It becomes disjointed and tinny, then stops altogether, suffocated into silence.

I swallow, then close the lid. As I do, a voice calls out to me from the other room. "Where are you?"

"I'm back here," I call to my friend.

"Are you doing okay?" she asks.

I hesitate, studying this piece of a life that no longer feels like my own. And I surprise myself with my answer. "Yeah, I'm okay."

She pauses, and I can hear her nodding. "I'll be out here when you're ready," she says.

I stare at the music box for another moment. It's a relic out of time, and perhaps for someone else, its pink ribbons and bright music would be a comfort. But for me, it's a piece of a life I left behind when I stepped out of those caves. The box no longer belongs to me.

I lean over and replace the toy where I found it—I'm careful to line it up with the outline in the carpet that was left by the ash. Then I begin to climb back through the mess of debris toward my friend. The box's music may have faded away, but we will not.

Despite everything that has happened, we are still here.

In the End, It Was Beautiful

I'VE BEEN LIVING OUT *here for years, and somehow I've only just started to notice how beautiful it all is.*

I surprise myself with how legible my handwriting is as I scratch the pencil against the paper. It's a souvenir pencil I found in a shop earlier today, which I sharpened with my utility knife, and a half-used pad of notepaper I found in an office somewhere toward the front of the subway station. The paper warped and rippled after growing damp at one point, but it's since dried. Now, it crinkles like the pages of an old tome every time I turn the page.

A heavy sigh joins the echo of the pages off the tile walls, and I turn toward its source, smiling. I pat my leg, and the brindle-coated shepherd looks up at me, then stands and walks the few feet over to where I sit, plopping his body weight heavily against me as he lies back down.

I couldn't say how long it's been, exactly. I lost track of that a long time ago. Or I stopped keeping track. It just doesn't seem all that important anymore without work or vacations or schedules to worry about. Sure, there are birthdays and holidays still—they don't stop just because the world did. But why do those need to be celebrated on certain days?

Just to be alive is worth celebrating.

I guess Simon gives me a sense of the time that has passed. When I found him as a puppy, in the corner of an old warehouse, he looked like a wet rag that needed to be rung out. He was shivering and damp and looked absolutely miserable. I remember taking him underneath my jacket to warm him up against my skin, bringing him back here with me.

That was . . . what? A year into all this?

Back then, I fed him chunks of beef stew in an old takeout container lid and let him lick the broth from my fingers. Now, he could probably eat two cans on his own. A few of his whiskers are starting to turn white on his muzzle, but he still acts like a puppy—

As if on cue, he turns and nudges my arm with his nose,

pushing my pencil across the page. I laugh and pause in my writing to weave my fingers into his long coat. His fur is softer than anything else I've felt in a long time. I've joked with myself before that I should collect it during the next shedding season to make a scarf. The clothes and blankets that have made it this long are all stiff with age and dirt, and their fibers crackle with each movement.

After a few minutes, he tucks his chin between his paws again and falls asleep, and I turn back to the half-used pad of paper in my lap.

I think people back then would've scoffed at me saying something like that. But we used to always find beauty in fragile things. Rare things. Flowers, precious jewels, crystal sculptures. Well, everything is fragile now. And it's all so precious—even an unopened can of stew, or a souvenir pencil.

Or this subway tunnel. I never would've bothered to look at it before. But after ... The mosaic on the back wall has started to chip and fall in places, especially below the water line from those storms last summer. But the blue tiles near the top still shimmer just a little, like beetle's wings. If I build our fire in the right place, the colors dance in the firelight, and the whole tunnel starts to glow. And when the fire fades, I get to lean back and watch the smoke curl upward through the skylight and disappear into the stars.

They're brighter too, now—the stars. I remember when my parents took me camping once, in the Badlands. I was really little, but I still remember how the sky was speckled with them, more than I'd ever known existed. I stared up at them for the longest time. I don't think I slept much that night—I remember getting in trouble the next morning since we were supposed to go on this long hike, and I could barely keep my eyes open. But I'd just wanted to watch them dance in the sky around us.

Now, though, I think they're even brighter. And the sky . . . How did I never realize the sky is not just a solid black but a whole pallet of colors? I've spent entire nights watching the stars carve their way through the swirls of inky blue, from one horizon to the next. And I don't get in trouble for it now.

In the mornings, Simon and I get to wake up with the rest of the earth and walk through the city. Sometimes I'll take my bike, if we're looking for food or supplies, but mostly these days I'll just walk. He'll trot alongside me, and we'll crunch through the leaves together, or he'll run off to play with some of the animals that are around. There's a family of raccoons that built a den in the old theater, and I swear the mom sees him as a nanny. Anyway, in a weird dog-parent kind of way, I'm happy that Simon has friends. (And they don't seem to be afraid of me, either, which has been an odd thing to get used to.) Every few days, I'll pick a new store to go through—I've made it all the way to 32nd Street by now, to that stationery store that had *all the pretty floral wrapping paper. (The name's faded off the sign, but I remember visiting it once.) And on our way back, I'll trek through that puddle of muck at the entrance to the station. I never did manage to clear it out like I'd hoped, but I don't really mind it anymore. I've grown to love the pattern of boot prints and paw prints crisscrossing over each other—a letter to the world that says we're still here.*

There was a time when leaving everything behind would've made me nervous. Meeting other people did, too. You never knew who was safe, or whether your home would still be there when you came back. But it doesn't really matter anymore. Every once in a while, I'll find a long-discarded mask trapped in the debris that's collected by the curb, or a treasure from some other survivors who have moved on—at least, I hope that's where they've gone. Maybe it's silly, but now, there are some days where I hope I'll go back to the subway station and find the remnants of my own survival raided. Just seeing a sign that there are other people still here, another set of boot prints in the mud to memorize . . .

But until I do, I'll keep looking for the beauty that's here with me. In the pencil and paper that I salvaged to write my thoughts. In the collection of treasures from other people's lives that are now part of my survival. In the ivy that's starting to trail down the escalator that leads to my camp, winding in lazy paths toward the light that's finally filtering through. In the way nature is slowly reclaiming what was here before, and already writing the next chapter. In Simon. In survival, and the hope that stubbornly survives with it.

My pencil is dull, and the fire has gone down to embers, so I don't have enough light to sharpen it. I set them both aside and lean back onto my bedding, and Simon rolls over beside me, pressing himself closer, his ear flicking lazily against my arm. As he sleeps, I stare up at the stars.

"And in you," I say. "You were here for a time. And that was beautiful too."

Part III: What's Found

Silence in the City, pt. 2

Day 1

T HE CHANGE HAPPENED IN less than a heartbeat.

I sat at a stoplight outside of the food pantry, drumming my fingers on the steering wheel and staring at the brake lights in front of me. My eyelids were heavy and my body stiff after having spent so many hours in the truck yesterday. But I was only a short drive from the hospital. I'd drop off my haul—crates of frozen, prepackaged food that I knew tasted about as good as the cardboard they came wrapped in—and then go get some actual food. I could taste it all now: runny eggs, crispy hash browns, sizzling bacon. My mouth was already watering. I reached for my thermos, focusing on my dreams of a breakfast that would make my cardiologist wince as I brought the lukewarm coffee to my lips.

Then the brake lights in front of me switched off. The

radio's music became static. A few cars in front of me, I heard a squeal and the jarring crunch of metal. The engine of my truck clicked a few times, as if cooling, then fell silent, taking the white noise of the radio with it.

My heartbeat pounded a steady rhythm in my ears, but otherwise, the entire world held its breath.

And then the screaming started.

People shouted, panic rising with the sound of their voices. I watched the car doors in front of me swing open, and I tentatively did the same, standing on the running board and leaning out into the street.

"My phone's dead!"

"Mine too!"

"Does anyone know what's going on?"

No one bothered replying; even the woman who'd asked knew the answer to her question. For some reason I couldn't place, my chest fluttered, and my stomach rolled over on itself, the hunger from a moment ago gone.

No one knew what was happening. Nor did we know then that, a few streets away, the generators for the hospital had stopped humming too.

Day 88

I'd lived too many years in that delivery truck, drinking watered-down coffee and staring at the painted lines on the interstate that traced from one end of the country to another. It was more than I should have had. About eight years ago, I'd fought through a stubborn flu that had left me tired and out of breath for a couple of weeks. My wife had insisted I go see someone; I had refused to spend the money. And then the bill had come due anyway, when that chest cold had turned into chest pains that put me in an ambulance to the ER. Now, a pacemaker kept my heart beating, and never-ending medical bills kept me driving.

Had.

The world I knew now was not the same one I'd lived in before.

I sat up, trying to rub away the pain in my chest, the heaviness that was too much of a reminder. The couch cushions and blankets I'd piled into a haphazard bed had shifted a little beneath me, and the room had grown a little colder in the night, but as usual, that wasn't what had woken me.

With a sigh, I tossed the blankets aside and moved closer to the fireplace, feeling for the box of matches I kept on the mantel. My stiff joints protested as I knelt down and fumbled through lighting some of the tinder still in the bottom, but after a few minutes of nursing the embers, a comforting crackle reached my ears. As the warm glow flicked through the room and across the walls, my eyes scanned the shelves that surrounded me.

It had only taken me a week or so after the blackout to make my way to the library. At first, I'd taken shelter in the food pantry, alongside the other survivors. Was it too early to call us that? Maybe, but it felt more and more accurate as the days stretched on without power or connection, and as people's panic began to take shape into something more sinister. Their voices began to fall more often into hushed tones and sideways glances, and their circles tightened around those they knew they could trust.

And no one knew me here, much less trusted me. Three months ago, I'd lived states away. I was a quiet, gruff old man who had never been much of one for making friends, especially now. And even if I had thought I could somehow make the journey home, there was nothing to go back to except a much too small house, which had been much too quiet and much too empty for the past three years.

So I'd journeyed deeper into the city.

I'd figured at first that the library would have another community of survivors. But when I came upon an empty, abandoned building instead, I realized how much better this was. Most of the food from my truck had been scavenged by those at the pantry in the first days, but I'd saved some for myself back at the beginning, and now, it was plenty to keep me fed through the winter, until I could plant some of what I'd found in the seed bank in one of the back rooms. There was plenty of water from the ten-gallon jugs that had been used to refill the water fountains in the study rooms, especially if I collected rainwater in the jugs that were empty, and there was warmth from the fireplace (and plenty of flyers and printer paper to burn before I would even need to touch the books).

Most importantly, here, I didn't need people to keep me company; I had thousands of stories for that.

The library was safe, and welcoming, and warm—especially with the fire now burning in the hearth. I was careful with rationing my supplies and restocking them when I could, and I figured if I stayed smart, I could carry on this way for as long as I needed to.

Yet the pain in my chest said otherwise.

I rubbed at the ache again, then stood up and moved back to my "bed," grunting softly as I reached for my pill bottle first, pouring one into my hand and swallowing it dry. Then I picked up my book. The pages of *The*

Tempest were soft and flicked quietly against my thumb as I opened up to the last page I'd read. I listened to the flutter of the pages, the hiss of the log I'd added to the fire to stoke it, the distant sound of an owl outside. My eyes scanned the words in the firelight, but I couldn't bring myself to actually read them. Nothing willed the thought away from my mind—of the deep ache that had woken me the past few nights, or the odd flutter that I'd felt ever since the world went quiet.

I didn't need the internet or doctors from before, or any of the countless books around me now, to tell me what I knew it meant.

My pacemaker's battery was dying. And so was I.

Day 127

I sat bolt upright in bed, sending the cushions and blankets sliding beneath me. This night, it wasn't my heart that woke me up. It was the sound of glass shattering somewhere in the distance.

I held my breath, my ears pricked for the sound I swore I'd heard. After a moment, when no other noise came, I threw the rest of the blankets off of me and pulled myself to my feet.

I'd grown too used to the quiet of the world these days to have dreamt it.

With no light to lead me, I padded down the hallways by memory, stepping as quietly as I could in my heavy-soled boots. I didn't even dare to breathe too deeply. I knew any number of things could've caused a broken window or a glass to shatter—an animal, a tree limb, a falling glass from the staff room I'd dubbed the kitchen. I'd been dismantling some of the bookshelves and furniture in the opposite end of the library to repurpose as other bits of furniture for my makeshift home; perhaps one of the boards had fallen over on a display case?

Could be, but I was worried about another, much more likely possibility.

I made a complete circle around the library without a sign of a broken case or a shattered window, but with the clouds from the day before still crowding out the moonlight, I only had the soles of my shoes by which to find it. As I rounded the corner back toward the library's main entrance, I had already relented to wait until the next morning and go back to bed.

As much as I hated the idea.

But then, as I drew closer to the glass double doors that had once welcomed people inside the library, I realized I could start to see vague shapes and shadows of the room in front of me. I pursed my lips, moving closer to the faint orange light that filtered in.

I didn't have to take many more steps before I saw what it was, though it took me a few moments longer to truly process it. The front entrance looked out onto a familiar street, which stretched all the way to a crudely built barricade of cars and a large delivery truck at the farthest edge of my vision. I'd never seen the barricade at night, but I could now. And I could see the building beside it—the flames licking out the windows and through the roof, sending black smoke into the air that mixed with the clouds lingering in the sky.

My heart sank. *All those people . . .* But there was nothing anyone could do—not in this world.

I heard no more glass breaking that night, but if I

listened closely, I could still hear the roar of the fire, even when I eventually turned and went back to bed.

Day 128

Although I went back to the study that night, I never fell back asleep. And once the first light of the morning began to illuminate the room around me from the high windows on the walls, I was up and searching once more for the broken glass.

On my second pass through the building, I finally found it—a small square windowpane smashed inward in the room I'd been gutting the day before. A jagged piece still poked out of the window frame, and the rest of the glass was scattered across the floor, casting small light beams along the ground as they reflected the sunlight. I bent down to study them, my knees creaking with the movement. The window that had been broken was tiny, barely taller than the crawl space I'd had underneath my house. A quick glance outside showed there were no animal prints in the mud or fallen branches.

And then I leaned back, and I saw the smear of crimson on the jagged corner that stuck out from the frame.

My heart hammered against my chest. I stood up quickly, whipping around to scan the rest of the room. I hadn't seen, hadn't heard any other proof of another person in the library. But I didn't need it. This was enough.

As quickly and quietly as I could, I crept back down the hall, cringing at each footfall that hit too heavily against the linoleum and each wheeze of my breath that left my lips. My lungs felt tight in my ribcage, my heart fluttering until I was almost dizzy. By the time I reached the study where I'd been staying, I leaned against the wall for support. Still, I ignored my body's warnings and pushed past the shake in my hands, easing the door open.

A man stood inside, his back to the door. His dark hair was just long enough to brush the tops of his ears and the back of his neck; I could tell he was younger. Fitter. Stronger. For a moment, I stood there, watching as he paced around my bed. He paused and nudged the ash in the fireplace with his foot, then picked up the matchbox on the mantel. He turned, spying the orange pill bottle tucked against the small stack of books on the floor. Kneeling, he picked it up, examining the label. And then he glanced up, his eyes meeting mine.

We froze, neither of us daring to move or even to blink. His jaw was set, a vein starting to bulge in his neck. My grip on the door tightened, both in preparation for what he would do and to keep myself upright. Slowly, he set the pill bottle back on the ground and began to stand, and I edged the door open farther, adrenaline sending my heart rate skyrocketing.

And then a second face, and a third, came into view.

The little girl's head barely cleared the tables that she hid behind at the back of the room. She stared at me with wide eyes as she peered out from behind one of the table's legs. Her mother stood beside her, her eyes and hair a perfect match to her daughter's. A bandage was tied around the top of her arm. One hand was tucked behind her back, and her gaze flicked from me to her husband and then to her daughter and back. Wordlessly, she used her other hand to wave the little girl over, then tucked her behind her back as well. It was then that I spotted the fourth face: a younger boy, peering out from between his mom's legs. He was even shorter than his sister, with a thumb planted firmly in his mouth.

In spite of the stars threatening to form at the edge of my vision, I softened. I met the father's gaze, then held up my hands by my face, showing him my empty palms.

"It's okay," I said. My voice was gravelly and nearly caught in my throat; I wasn't exactly sure when I'd last spoken. "Let me just . . ." I pointed toward the pill bottle, hoping he understood.

The man glanced at his wife, then nodded, stepping back from the bed.

Slowly, I came into the room, then moved toward the same pile, not even making eye contact. I grabbed the pill bottle and my latest book off the top of the pile—*Lord of the Flies*—and tucked them both inside my jacket. I stifled a cough behind my fist as I stood, then ducked my head, shuffling back out of the room.

I closed the door behind me, then moved to the opposite wall, leaning my forehead against it as I tried to steady myself. After an agonizing minute, the adrenaline coursing through my veins began to ease, but something else seemed to coil around my chest in its place. It took me a moment to name it, in between lungfuls of air and careful movements as I tried to slow my racing heart.

It was dread.

Day 151

I used the broken-down furniture in the far room to board up the smashed window and craft a new home for myself, of sorts. A few cushioned benches and coats from the lost and found made a passable place to sleep, at least until I could scrounge up a better option. The room was colder and much draftier than the other had been—the shattered windowpane and shoddy patch job I'd given it hardly helped—but I still had a couple of weeks before the cold truly set in. I could find a way to stay warm before then . . . or hope my new neighbors were willing to take in a guest.

Somehow, that didn't seem likely. A couple of weeks had passed since the family had arrived, but they might as well have been ghosts haunting the building for how much I'd seen of them. Or maybe I was the ghost haunting them. When I walked the halls during the day, I could sometimes hear their hushed mutters carrying through the vents, falling silent when I drew nearer to their door. I'd tried extending an olive branch on that first day, after the shock of the situation had worn off. I'd gone to the children's corner and dusted off a teddy bear that had been forgotten, leaving it outside the door to the study. It had been gone the next day, though I never saw the face of the person who took it.

The only face I did see was the father's, a week later as I was taking stock of my food. He wandered into the staff room as I counted my provisions: mostly cans of beans and vegetables and cups of fruit suspended in sticky syrup. Like before, we froze when we saw each other. Then, hesitantly, he moved to the other end of the room, beginning to fill up a water bottle with the ten-gallon jug on the wall.

My heart rate spiked as I started to collect my food and tuck it back on the shelves. "Sorry," I muttered, my gruff voice more of a growl in the small space than I'd intended it to be. I tried forcing myself to slow down, the world around me starting to teeter. I took a deep breath, blowing it out slowly as I grabbed the counter.

From where he stood, the man turned, studying me. His gaze drifted from my face to the shelves where my food was stored, then back to his water jug. He continued for a few more seconds, then screwed the lid back on his bottle and left, the jug's gurgling drowning out his footsteps. His expression was unreadable.

I wasn't sure why, but I suddenly felt so exposed. So *vulnerable*. I hadn't wanted to hide my supplies from the others, especially with little kids in the mix. But what I wouldn't have given now for a padlock to place on the door.

When my heart stopped racing and the black eased back from where it had built at the edges of my vision, I grabbed a few more cans than were necessary for dinner that night and took them back to my corner of the building.

It was a few hours later when the feeling returned—the fluttering in my chest, the fogginess in my head. I'd been lying in bed, staring into the pitch black with wide eyes as I thought about the food stores I'd counted earlier. Even if I had still been alone, the cans I had in the staff room were not enough to last through the winter. With the others living here now, it added stress to the water supply, and this side of the building was letting in too much air for me to stay warm . . .

The thought of scavenging for supplies sent my heart racing and my stomach sinking. I'd put it off, worried about the danger and whether I'd be able to find anything. And now it was colder and darker. The food pantry was gone. And my health was worse. What if I had waited too long?

After a few minutes, I tried to will the thoughts away. It did me no good to think about them tonight. I'd come up with a plan tomorrow, starting with finding another room where I could sleep. I shivered, tugging my coat closed around my neck, and closed my eyes.

The fluttering in my chest became a stutter, one that

I could feel through my ribcage. I pressed a hand to my sternum, willing myself to search for my pill bottle with the other. My fingers fumbled around the lighter I'd found to light my way at night, my worn-out copy of *The Road* . . .

And nothing else. The pill bottle wasn't there.

I sat up, the movement sparking a dull ache behind the palm on my chest. I tried to think back through the day, retrace my steps until I could see it in my memory. Finally, I remembered the counter in the staff room. I'd taken it in there and set it by the sink, then forgotten it in my rush to leave.

It was three hallways away, with only faint starlight and a lighter to guide me.

Trying to take in a breath, I palmed the lighter and heaved myself to my feet, striking it twice before the spark caught into a flame. Holding it in front of me like a candle, I steadied myself against the bookcase and began to walk.

My pace was agonizingly slow, each step causing my vision to cloud and the ache in my chest to sharpen. My footsteps were no longer the careful, quiet tiptoe they'd been before, though I couldn't tell how loud they were—a ringing had started in my ears that drowned out everything else. Several times, my fingers slipped on the lighter, or my balance started to tip, and I leaned against the wall for support until I could continue.

By the time I finally made it to the staff room, the pain had radiated into my arm, until it almost felt heavy. I rested it on the counter instead and leaned against it, flicking the lighter again until its warm light cast color back into the room.

The pill bottle wasn't where I'd left it. I panned the flame down the length of the counter, hoping I'd catch a glimpse of the orange plastic in the glow, but there was nothing except shadows dancing in the light.

The air left my lungs in a huff. Suddenly, my knees buckled, and I dropped the lighter, hearing it clatter somewhere by my feet. I couldn't tell if it was my heart giving out or my hope, but whichever it was left an empty feeling in its wake. Was this the end?

The answer to my question came with the sound of quiet footfalls, padding softly in the hallway outside as my eyes drifted closed.

Day 152

"Hey, easy now." The whisper reached through the fog in my head first, though I couldn't seem to place it. I opened my eyes, squinting as I waited for them to focus.

"Can you hear me, sir?"

It was the father of the other family in the library, staring down at me. His hair hung down in his eyes, looking even longer with his eyebrows drawn up the way they were. After a moment, I nodded.

He nodded back, then placed a hand gently on my shoulder. "You took a tumble back in the staff room, but I figured you were after those pills you carry. I found them up in the cabinet and gave you one." He let out a shaky breath. "You scared me there."

"Sca—" I gave a weak cough and tried again. "Scared you?"

"Mm-hmm." The man glanced back behind his shoulder, then turned to face me again. "Do you think you can walk?"

The man helped me back to the study, matching his steps with my own snail pace. Once inside, he brought me over to a bench in the far corner, a small pile of blankets already stretched across it. The man's family slept huddled on the pile of cushions by the fireplace.

"I can light the fire if you need," he offered, helping me settle on the makeshift bed. I shook my head.

"Do you have water?"

He helped steady my quivering hands with his own as I drank, the water soothing the roughness in my throat. Once I was finished, he screwed the cap back on the bottle and set it aside, not meeting my eyes.

"I didn't know what to make of you at first," he admitted. "An outsider broke into the shelter where we were before, and she . . . killed a girl . . ."

I waited, trying to piece together what he was saying.

"I didn't know if it was you, or what you would do to us when you found us here. And then when you let us stay, I . . ." He paused, shaking his head and giving a grim chuckle. "My wife said you were trying to be nice. And I didn't believe her." He looked up, meeting my eyes. "Why didn't I believe her?"

I stayed silent, my gaze drifting as I digested all of it. "You were living in the shelter before?" The dad nodded, and I met his gaze. "I didn't know whether to trust you at first either," I admitted.

"For a minute," he said, and there was a slight waver in his voice, "when I heard you tonight, I thought about not helping. Does that mean I'm just as bad as them?"

I studied him for a moment. "We've both been trying to survive since this whole thing started," I finally said.

"But that's not enough anymore."

I fell asleep when the sky was just beginning to lighten in the windows, and awoke some time later to the warm glow of a fire crackling in the hearth. I sat up slowly, making sure I had my bearings, then wrapped a blanket around my shoulders and moved closer to the fireplace.

The man's wife smiled softly as I approached. "How are you feeling this morning?" She asked. Her voice was like silk.

I cleared my throat, a bit self-conscious. "Better, thank you."

Her husband came through the door just then, a small package in his hand. He moved around the couch and bent down to kiss her cheek, then turned to me. "Are you hungry at all? We have more than enough." He held up the package—it was a bag of dried noodles.

"I don't want to impose," I started, but the woman cut me off.

"We broke into your home and took your bed," she said, ducking her head a little as her cheeks flushed. "If anyone is an imposition, it's us."

"Not at all."

As her husband began to cook, the woman looked at

something behind me, then smiled, gesturing for someone to come closer. "It's okay. Come here."

A second passed, and then the two smallest members of the family moved past me, taking seats on either side of their mother. The little boy tugged at the cardigan she wore, using it to hide half his face.

"It's okay," I said softly. "I promise I'm nice."

The mom turned to her son, gently taking her sweater out of his hands and revealing his face. "Why don't you show him the book we were reading?" she asked. The little boy nodded, running to somewhere at the back of the room and returning a moment later with a small worn paperback. He handed it to his mom, and she held it out for me to see. "They saw it in your stack of books and insisted I read it to them."

I read the title and smiled. *The Swiss Family Robinson.* I turned to the children. "That's always been one of my favorites," I whispered. I winked at them, and the little girl giggled. She turned to her mom.

"Can we read some?" she asked.

"After breakfast," the mom answered, then glanced at me. "You don't mind a bit of story time, do you?"

"There's nothing I'd love more."

As she turned back to her husband to say something, and her son began flipping through the pages of their book, I realized how much I'd missed this—these sounds, this warmth. I'd been missing it even before the world went quiet, I realized. The thought left a funny feeling in my chest, different to all the ones I'd felt before.

"Mommy said your heart hurt," said a sing-songy voice beside me, breaking into my thoughts. I turned to see the little girl staring up at me, hugging something just under her chin as she spoke. It took me a second to recognize it: a small brown teddy bear. The one I'd left here when they'd first arrived.

"It did," I finally told her. "But I'm feeling a lot better now."

Last Christmas

"**I** CAN'T BELIEVE YOU'RE actually doing this."

"You didn't have to come," I reminded him.

My best friend, Jonah, just gave me a sideways glance as we walked. I shrugged, then turned back to the road ahead.

"I'm not waiting around back at the complex, knowing you are willingly and purposefully going back there, for . . . what is it again, exactly?"

I sighed. "A tin of sewing supplies. You remember those cookie tins that never actually had any cookies in them?"

Jonah nodded. "Right. Adam, you do know we could probably raid any of these homes and find exactly what's in that tin? Without facing our imminent deaths?"

"I know, I know, but it was Macy's grandmother's tin. It's got . . ." I waved my hands, searching for the right word. "Sentimental value."

"Uh-huh. Personally, I think our lives have sentimental value." Jonah shrugged his shoulders up near his ears, scuffing his boot against the ground. "And I'd like to remind you that Macy's grandmother's tin is currently guarded by your ex-girlfriend," he whined.

I pursed my lips. If I opened them again, I knew I'd admit that what we were doing was dumb. Incredibly dumb. But hey, love makes you do dumb things.

Like walk all the way back to your crush's old house with your best friend, without telling anyone else at the complex where you're going, to retrieve an old sewing kit in the middle of the zombie apocalypse.

Yeah, okay, even I could hear it. But it was almost Christmas, which was hard enough to stomach these days. It was also almost a year since Macy had lost *her* best friend. I wanted to do something to cheer her up, show her I was thinking about her. And sure, maybe win some brownie points with her, too. After all, it had also been about a year since I'd left my ex, and I'd grown to really like Macy. The apocalypse was lonely enough already, and I was tired of being alone.

I wasn't truly alone, of course. Macy, Jonah, and

I—we'd been about the same age when we'd come to the complex, and we'd quickly bonded with the other kids there. There were six of us now, five years in, but we agreed that was pretty good odds considering all we'd lived through. That group was how I'd gotten this idea in the first place. Franklin had come back from scouting the other day with a bundle of old wire and a goofy grin on his face. We'd given him weird looks at first, until he'd managed to untangle the wire. "Christmas lights!" he'd announced proudly. "We can't light them, but I figured we could hang them up under the bridge and make it a bit cheerier."

And thus, the idea for Christmas in the apocalypse was born.

"You want to know what I'm getting Grayson?" Jonah continued. "A new knife. It's small, practical—"

"Sewing supplies are practical," I reminded him. I reached over and tapped the patch he'd just sewn on the sleeve of his jacket. He mumbled something else unintelligible.

His complaints didn't bother me. I'd known Jonah long enough that I recognized when he was nervous. The fact that he was still beside me showed the kind of friend he was—and secretly, I was really glad he was here to back me up. Even if it did mean tolerating a bit of grumbling along the way.

"There it is," I said, cutting Jonah's rambling off mid-sentence. I nodded toward the house at the end of the cul-de-sac.

He took a deep breath. "How do you want to do this?"

"Quietly," I answered. I knelt into a crouch and gestured for Jonah to follow. At this point, I knew we were both tuned in to the world around us. We'd gotten used to the soft growls of the undead over the years, but neighborhoods like this one were always especially dangerous—plenty of hiding spaces for them to lurk, and plenty of buildings that you couldn't be sure had been cleared. Some houses likely still had tenants from the beginning of the outbreak holed up inside of them.

We crawled along the side of the house until we reached a window toward the back. The glass had a solid coating of grime on the outside, but I used my sleeve to clear away what I could and tried to peer inside. I turned back to Jonah. *Looks clear,* I mouthed. He nodded and reached into his coat pocket, pulling out a utility knife. He moved up beside me and worked the blade into the crevice, deftly popping the lock. He carefully slid the window open and gestured for me to climb inside.

***

The room I was in was coated in a layer of dust, and my

feet kicked up a cloud of it as I landed on the carpet, forcing me to swallow a cough. The air smelled stale, with the faint, sickly sweet scent of rot, but otherwise, the house looked basically untouched. I gave Jonah the all-good signal, then glanced around the room as he climbed in behind me. Everything was varying shades of pink, from the walls to the bedspread. A pile of stuffed animals in one corner and a boy band poster tacked up on the back of the bedroom door told me I'd guessed right as to whose room this had been.

"This is the girl you have a crush on?" Jonah whispered, a grin playing across his face.

I gave him a light shove. "Hey, she was, like, ten. Besides, we both know what you were like back then." I nodded toward the door. "Her parents' room should be just across the hall."

We approached the hallway the same way we had the window, with Jonah manning the door while I stepped out to make sure the coast was clear. This time, I reached into my pocket and brought out my own knife, holding it in front of me as I stepped out.

Just like the bedroom, it was empty.

Once we made sure there weren't any unwelcome visitors in Macy's parents' bedroom, Jonah and I shut the door behind us to search. We riffled through the closet, both nightstands, and even the chest at the foot of the bed that housed extra pillows and blankets. No tin.

"Did Macy ever say *where* the tin was?" Jonah whispered at one point, climbing onto a storage bin to look at the top shelf of the closet.

"No. And I couldn't think of how to ask without giving away the surprise."

"It'll be a surprise if we find it," he muttered, climbing back down and dusting his palms on his pants. "No dice. Where to next?"

My face twisted into a grimace. "These are the only two bedrooms on this side of the house. Then it's just the linen closet, the bathroom off of the living room, and . . ."

"The kitchen?" Jonah guessed.

"Yeah."

He pursed his lips, thinking. Then, he grabbed his knife and headed toward the door. "Let's hope Mrs. Donnelly kept her sewing kit with the toilet paper."

<hr />

Mrs. Donnelly did not, in fact, keep her sewing kit with the toilet paper. Nor did she tuck it away in the linen closet, which I'd really been hoping for. The basement was a maze, I knew, and probably plenty dangerous, but I really doubted the tin was going to be down there. Which meant there was one room left to check.

The Donnellys' kitchen had a partition that separated it from the rest of the house, and the only entrance into it had been blocked off with a tired old mattress—for good reason. Creeping up on it now, I could still see where a reddish-brown stain had seeped along the bottom and soaked into the fibers.

At this point, I was really taking Jonah's earlier questions to heart. I mean, I liked Macy, but did I really like her *this* much?

Unfortunately for me, Jonah had left his hesitations somewhere at the back of the house. Before I could change my mind, he clenched the blade of his knife in his teeth and placed both hands on the mattress, watching for my signal.

I let out a small breath and stretched my neck, getting into a fighting stance. I waited another second, then nodded before I had a chance to think about what we were doing.

Jonah pulled the mattress to the side, and I steeled myself.

There was nothing.

Jonah paused, the mattress three-quarters of the way clear of the entryway. He leaned around the mattress. "Where'd she go?" he asked, his teeth still clenched around his knife.

My heart fluttered. "I don't know," I whispered back.

Could I really be this lucky?

Taking his knife from his teeth, he stepped back around the mattress to peer around the corner. "Maybe she got out?" he asked, his voice a little louder this time. "I mean she . . ." The word "she" morphed into a curse, then a string of curses as the mattress tumbled over on top of him, sending his knife clattering to the floor. An awkwardly shuffling foot kicked it farther out of reach, and my eyes trailed up to a very familiar graying, gaunt face.

Julia. Macy's best friend, and my ex-girlfriend.

Well, the zombified version of her.

Okay, before I continue, a quick bit of clarification. First, Julia and I broke up before she was bitten. I'm not that heartless. We'd been growing apart for a while—or at least, that's what she'd said. Unfortunately, that had been the moment I'd decided to tell her I loved her, and she'd stormed off with Macy.

I'd assumed they went somewhere else in the complex. If I'd known they were coming back here . . .

Anyway, second bit of clarification: Yes, I admit I make poor decisions when it comes to relationships. I'm a hopeless romantic who's also facing a quickly dwindling dating pool. Sue me.

When I finally realized where they'd gone—and by the time I managed to make it here without running into any of Macy's undead neighbors—it had already been too late. Macy had tried bandaging Julia's leg, but we could already see the infection spreading. Julia told us to block her in the kitchen and get out while we still could, so we'd said our goodbyes while pushing the mattress into place.

The mattress that was now pinning Jonah to the ground, out of reach of his only weapon, while Julia stared at me.

For a moment, she just stood there. I was frozen in place. I hadn't ever been this close to one of them for this long, especially without it attacking, and I had no idea what to do. I didn't even want to breathe in case it would startle her. But also, it was *her*. Her hair was a bit unkempt but still in its long, dark braid. Her eyes were a glassy brown, and her cheekbones protruded a bit more—*because, you know, she's dead*, I reminded myself.

From the corner of my eye, I could see Jonah trying to wriggle free, one arm out and reaching desperately for his knife. If I could just keep her eyes on me, maybe I could buy him some time. With Julia still staring at me, I started to take a slow step backward, then another . . .

Then Jonah's knife scraped along the hardwood as he managed to grab hold of it, and whatever trance Julia had been in lifted. She let out an awful raspy hiss and stumbled toward me, and I ducked and fell out of the way, trying to force my feet to move. I reached into my pocket for my knife, but then I felt her fingers wrapping around my arm, pulling me closer to her. I twisted around, pushing her backward desperately with my forearm against her collarbone.

"A little help?!" I shouted, terror leaching into my voice.

"I'm trying!" Jonah yelled. "My foot is . . . ergh—"

I gritted my teeth at the sight of Julia's gaping mouth. Reaching my leg up, I kneed her away with as much force as I could, then ran over to the mattress and bent down to leverage it off Jonah.

"For a second there, it looked like she recognized you," he said breathlessly, crawling out and scrambling to his feet.

"Yeah, I don't think so." I let the mattress fall with a heavy *thump*, kicking a cloud of dust into the air. "How do we get out of here?"

"Can we make it to the front door?" he asked.

Julia answered that one, giving another raspy yell from near the front entryway as she jerkily got to her feet. We both raised our knives—and probably both wished for something with a little more range—as she started toward us, arms outstretched.

I had just enough time to jump to the side and Jonah to move back into the kitchen before she was on top of us, this time going for Jonah's throat. I ran in behind her, wrapping my arm around her torso and trying to haul her off him.

"Adam! Look!"

"I'm a little busy!" I reminded him.

He said something else, but it was drowned out by the gurgling rasps that Julia was making. The way she was twisted, if I let go to try to use my knife, she and I were going to have matching bite marks.

"What?"

"The tin!"

My eyes widened. "Grab it!" I heard shuffling in the kitchen but didn't dare look. I turned back to Julia, her teeth reaching dangerously close to my shoulder. Mustering all the strength I could, I shoved against her, my shoulder shoving into her and sending her sprawling. Jonah ran up just then, a faded blue shortbread tin tucked under his arm.

Neither of us waited for an invitation. Together, we bolted for the front door, flinging it open and feeling the cold wind smack us in the face as we found our way outside. I slammed the door shut behind us, then bent over, coughing. My lungs burned, and I could hear my blood pounding in my ears.

"I never want to run into one of your old girlfriends again," Jonah sputtered, still gasping for breath.

I wanted to make a snide comment back, but my brain wouldn't find one. Instead, I nodded toward the tin under his arm wordlessly. He handed it over without looking up.

"Thanks," I muttered.

"Don't mention it." Pushing against his knees, he straightened, pointing toward the street. "We probably need to get moving."

"Yeah, we definitely woke some of them up."

Jonah nodded, then let out a final breath, starting back toward the complex. Tucking the tin safely beneath my arm, I followed close behind him.

A few days later, six survivors sat around a crackling fire beneath a small archway toward the back of the complex. A string of lights arced haphazardly along the back wall, and someone had even twisted holly branches into a small wreath in the center.

My heart raced as I felt Macy shift closer to me, her

fingertips lightly brushing mine. We watched as the others exchanged their gifts: Franklin gave Kamiko batteries for her watch, Kamiko had made cookies for everyone with real chocolate, and Jonah had found some old comics to add to the group's "library." Even in the firelight, I could see Jonah blushing as he gave Grayson the knife he'd bought him from the commissary. I had to admit, it was a nice knife.

And then my turn came, and everyone faced me. My heart fluttered. "Macy," I started. She turned to me, her eyes widening ever so slightly. "First, I need to say that Jonah helped me with your gift—"

"Nearly died for it," he muttered, but he wore a grin.

I chuckled. "Yeah, fair. But I really wanted it to be special." I smiled, then reached for my jacket behind me, pulling out the tin, a piece of paper taped on top.

Macy gasped. "Is that . . . ?" Her eyes widened, and she looked at me. "Adam, tell me you didn't go back there just for me."

"We did," Jonah confirmed.

I shrugged, looking down at the ground. Now I was the one blushing. "I wanted it to be special."

"This is . . . more than special. I can't believe it." She fell silent, and I looked up, watching as she studied the note I'd taped to the top. It was short but to the point, and she bit her lip to hide a smile.

I love you, Macy. Merry Christmas.

"What is it?" Kamiko finally asked, her sing-song voice breaking the silence. Macy looked up, beaming.

"It's my grandmother's sewing supplies. She was the one who taught me to sew." She began to open the tin as she spoke. "We'd left these back at my house when everything started, but with all the patchwork I've been doing recently . . ."

I had caught Jonah's gaze from across the circle as she spoke, but a frown on his face and Macy's sudden silence brought my attention back to her. She stared at the tin for a moment, her eyebrows drawn together.

And then she started laughing.

"What? What is it?" I asked. I reached over, tilting the tin in my direction so I could peer inside. Macy didn't even notice; she was too busy wiping tears from the corners of her eyes.

My heart sank. Cookies. The tin was full of cookies.

"No, wait. That's not right!" I turned to Jonah, and he shrugged, looking as confused as I felt. "You said your grandmother's supplies were in an old cookie tin," I said to Macy.

It took her a moment to compose herself enough to speak, but then she nodded. "They are. They're in a tin just like this in the laundry room."

The laundry room. Which was just to the right of the

stairs that led down to the basement. Of course.

"Macy, I'm so sorry. I didn't—"

"Are you kidding me? You risked your life for this. For me." She smiled, her eyes looking misty in the firelight as they held my gaze. "Thank you."

She leaned in, wrapping her arms around me in a tight hug, and butterflies swarmed my stomach. She tilted her head so her lips were next to my ear. "I love you too," she whispered, so only I could hear.

As she pulled away, my heart was racing—for once, not because I was fighting for my life. And as Macy began passing crumbly shortbread around the circle of friends, I realized with certainty that even with all the years I'd celebrated it before, even if it was the last time I would ever celebrate the holiday, this was the happiest Christmas of my life.

"Merry Christmas, everyone," Macy said, raising her cookie as a toast.

"Merry Christmas!" we all echoed.

"But I'm just putting this out there," Jonah said. "If we do this again next year, I'm not going back to that house for the right tin."

Ship of Theseus

T HE GIRL DID NOT know how long she had been adrift.

The albatrosses woke her up, like they did every morning. They made their high-pitched trills, telling her it was time for a new day to start, that it was time to get up and start tying down the sails and helping Mother prepare breakfast. *But there are no sails to tie down today*, she wanted to tell them. *No Mother to bring me food or water*.

She was desperate for water, especially—not the kind that the fish swam in outside the ship and that she floated in now, but the sweeter kind that you could drink. Her lips were cracked and sore, and her skin and throat felt tight. Salt was caked in her hair and her clothes, making them stiff and scratchy, and spots of white dotted the collection of boards that had become her life raft. She traced them with her finger as she floated, the way she used to do on the deck of the ship.

She wasn't really sure what she was supposed to do

now. She had always had the ship—it was all she'd ever known. She'd had campouts on the deck with the others on board, watching the stars. She'd hidden beneath its beams from the storms and the sun that baked her now. She'd watched Father repair the leaks in the hull by heating the colorful hard rocks that sometimes showed up in the fish's stomachs, and she'd learned to swim off its edge with her friends when she'd been old enough. But then the wave had crashed down, and . . .

She closed her eyes tightly. She didn't want to think about the storm. She just wanted water. She wanted fresh fish eggs, like Mother used to sneak her when she woke up early enough.

She just wanted the sky to be dark again, so she could go back to sleep.

___

The girl did wake some time later to a darkness, but not the one she'd expected. When she opened her eyes, she frowned, rubbing at them with a small fist. The shadow that moved over her raft made it cooler, bringing a bit of relief to the red burns and scrapes that had formed from her time in the water. With careful movements, and pushing some of the colorful bits that floated beside her out of the way, she turned over to rest her back against the boards. And then she frowned some more.

The ship was like hers, but it wasn't. This one had different sails, and a pointed piece at the front that jutted out over the water, and a white circular tube that reminded her of a fish eye dragging a wake into the clutter that floated beside it. It created small waves that slapped her legs as it bobbed up and down a few paces away. And as she watched it, a noise came from somewhere above her. She turned her face toward it, and she saw another girl standing there, watching her.

None of it made any sense. There weren't other ships—just hers, with Mother and Father and the other kids and their parents. She must've been dreaming. Yes, that was it.

The girl on the raft turned back onto her stomach, the water lapping over her itchy and blistered arms, and closed her eyes again.

When the girl from the raft awoke a third time, she was not on a raft, or even in the water. As she blinked her eyes hard to wait for them to adjust, she startled at the feeling of something thin and papery wrapped around each of her arms and legs, and at the pile of cloth on top of her. It reminded her of the time the sail had come loose in the wind and tangled around her until one of the men had come to help. She threw the cloth onto the floor and began peeling at the strange wrappings on her limbs, working her fingers frantically at the edges.

Suddenly, someone was beside her, placing their hand on hers. The girl looked up. It was a woman, with bronze skin and dark hair woven into a single strand. She met the girl's gaze, her eyebrows turning upward, then eased her back onto the cot, her lips moving in a strange series of sounds. Then, she reached over to a table beside her and passed her a small bowl.

The girl looked at the bowl for a moment, water sloshing around in the bottom, then at the woman. The woman frowned, then held her hands in a circle and mimed tipping the bowl to her lips. Suddenly, the girl got the idea. She mirrored the woman, drinking the cool water in two greedy swallows. It soothed her throat and washed away the dusty feeling on her tongue. She held the bowl out to the woman again, hoping for more.

The woman smiled, and the girl felt a flutter of pride in her belly at having guessed right. Then she watched as the woman stood and carried the bowl away.

The girl waved a hand, trying to get the woman's attention, but she disappeared around a corner on the far side of the room before she could. The girl's shoulders drooped. They'd always had to ration water for food and cleaning, but she was still thirsty. She glanced around, searching for a water barrel like they'd had on the rooms in her ship. But here, everything looked strange—piles of cloth on the cots and posts holding the beds off the floor, odd glass housing around their lamps that cast weird shadows across the beams in the room. Then she met the eyes of another girl watching her from the corner—the same girl she'd seen on the side of the ship before. She looked a lot like the woman, with dark hair piled atop her head and dark eyes that glinted at her from the shadows.

The two stared at each other for a moment, the new girl tipping her head to the side. It was enough for the girl to feel itchy again, and to start to squirm underneath the uncomfortable gaze. But then, the woman reappeared, the bowl in her hands again. She made another series of odd sounds, and the girl's observer ran off, leaving her to drink her water in peace.

The girl from the raft stayed in the room with the raised cots for a couple more days before the woman removed the wrappings from her limbs and let her wash away the goop smeared underneath them, and another day still before she was able to leave and wander the ship with the others. There were a lot more people here than she'd ever had on her own ship, and they all made the same strange noises to each other as the woman and the girl had. The boat itself was also odd, the girl learned—the colorful things that floated in the water and that her father had used to repair their hull were all around, sometimes replacing entire pieces of the ship. Up close, the sail was even a patchwork of colors, made up of several tarps stitched together tightly. She went over and inspected it once, but they had tied it down all wrong, and someone had shouted at her when she'd tried to fix it. She didn't try again.

Most of her days she spent in the woman's shadow, watching her play with other children in other parts of the ship or make concoctions in the kitchens with seaweed, various powders, and what looked like green slime. She called herself Lyra, the girl eventually learned, after the woman pointed at herself several times and made the sounds repeatedly. She pointed at the girl and said something else, her forehead wrinkled in a question, but the girl made the gesture for "I don't understand." Her family had always used their hands to talk to one another—it was how they could understand each other even over the crash of the waves against the hull.

Where the girl followed Lyra, the other girl that looked like Lyra—she was called Kai—followed them both. She never made as many noises as the others, hiding in the shadows when she could and always tipping her head at the girl when she used her hands to speak or stumbled at doing things the way Lyra wanted. She couldn't tell if Kai was fascinated by her or scared of her, and she couldn't decide which way she felt about Kai, either.

The three of them went everywhere together, though, even to the kitchens at mealtimes. The girl had turned her nose up at the food at first, until the growling of her stomach had pained her enough to try it. Their food was tough to chew and hurt her teeth—nothing like the fresh fish she'd watched Mother slice into pieces for the rest of the ship. It had taken the girl a while to understand how she was even meant to eat it that first day, her eyes scanning the room as people scraped the dried fish skin clean with their teeth. She'd still been gnawing on it when Lyra had tapped her arm, shaking her head at her and frowning. The girl had glanced around the room then, realizing everyone had stopped eating and stood beside their seats, waiting for something. She'd looked around the room, then up at an older man who now stood beside her, his beard speckled with flecks of silver. He glared at her and said something—of course, she didn't understand what—then stumbled away toward the front of the room. That was when the girl noticed how his feet shuffled in a strange way, and how his hands shook. She felt her cheeks redden, and her stomach twist in embarrassment. She pushed the rest of her dried fish over to Kai.

Nighttime, though—that was the worst, the girl had decided. When the sky darkened and it was time to sleep, everyone funneled belowdecks, into a long room lined with too-soft cots on either side. While everyone else snored and sighed, the girl's eyes stayed wide awake, staring at the lone lamp that hung near the stairs in the center of the room. By the time her third night came around, she felt as if the walls would squish her, and the stale, musty air made her nose wrinkle. After what felt like hours, she turned to Lyra and Kai's cot beside her and watched for a moment as their chests rose and fell in rhythm with the rocking of the ship. Satisfied they were asleep, she gathered the sheet that reminded her of her ship's sails and dragged it up the stairs to the deck.

Once the moonlight and fresh sea air washed over her, the girl sighed. She spread her sheet in front of the main mast, lay down on top of it, and stared up at the sky. The stars, at least, were familiar. They were the same ones she'd stared at every night that she could remember, her mother and father pointing out shapes in them as they lay on either side of her. But they were the only thing on this ship that reminded her of home.

As more weeks passed, the girl could tell her mood was growing sour. She didn't care. Instead of following

Lyra around while she did her chores, she sulked against the railing of the ship, watching the horizon bob up and down while the waves rocked against their hull. At mealtimes, she waited for the elders to eat, then tore at the fish skin angrily with her teeth, imagining it was all the things she hated about her new home. And at night, she still waited for the others to fall asleep, then took her sheet up to the deck to sleep there instead.

She grew especially angry with Kai, who seemed oblivious to her efforts to be left alone. She began to sit beside her at the ship's railing, scooting closer every time the girl shuffled away. She tried to mimic the girl's gestures when she'd sign to herself, and wore a proud smile when she waved at the girl one day to get her attention. She pointed at herself. "Kai," she said. Then she pointed at the girl, signing "I don't understand."

The girl sighed loudly and rolled her eyes, turning away.

It was when she woke up with the girl at night, however, that she became especially cross. "No!" she whispered to Kai as the girl gathered a blanket as if to follow the girl up the stairs. (That was one of the few sounds she had managed to learn.) She shook her head and signed the word, too, as if to emphasize her point, then dragged her sheet up top like always.

This night, the stars were blanketed by a layer of clouds

119

and fog, but the girl didn't mind. She curled herself up in a ball and huffed as she closed her eyes. Her forehead was still wrinkled in a frown as she fell asleep.

She wasn't sure how much later it was when she awoke. The sky was still dark, but the air felt different now, making her hair stand on end. The waves sounded more frantic as they beat against the ship, and the wind rippled through her sheet, tossing her straw-colored hair into her face.

The girl's heart pounded against her chest, and she tried to gather her sheet into her arms to carry it back downstairs. But before she could grab it, another gust of wind ripped it from her fingers, carrying it high above her head. She ran after it, a cry escaping her throat. But her fingers just brushed the edge before it drifted down to the surface of the water.

Her lip quivered, and she turned back toward the stairs to go belowdecks. She wasn't sure how she'd explain to Lyra how her sheet had gone missing, but she could only hope the woman wouldn't be angry with her. Just as she reached the top step, however, she stiffened, her eyes wide. Lightning lit the sky a brilliant white, and thunder rumbled.

Just as it had the night her ship had sunk.

The girl couldn't think, couldn't even breathe. She sank to the floor, tears stinging her eyes for the first time since she'd been aboard. Her shoulders quivered, and the images of the wave crashing over the sides flashed on the insides of her eyelids.

Then a pair of warm arms wrapped around her, squeezing her close. For once, this was a gesture she recognized. She wrapped her arms around the other person, holding tightly, her tears dampening her cheeks as if they were raindrops.

Kai eventually coaxed the girl back beneath the deck, and the two stayed awake throughout the storm, listening to the rain patter against the boards and feeling the waves break against the boat. The girl shivered every once in a while when thunder rumbled or a loud wave reached their ears, but for the most part, she was silent; her tears had turned into soft hiccups and the occasional sniffle.

Eventually, the storm broke, and a soft light filtered down into the room from the top of the stairs. Kai reached over and took the girl's hand, then slowly led her back toward the staircase. She didn't hesitate the way Kai had expected her to—she rubbed a fist against her eyes, only a little puffy from her tears and lack of sleep, then followed her up top.

As the two reached the deck, they blinked in the early

morning sunlight, squinting toward the horizon. Filtering through the remnants of last night's storm clouds, the sunlight turned the sky into a sea of brilliant pinks and hazy purples; the colors reflected off the ocean's surface, mixing with the bright-blue ripples that matched the girl's wide eyes. The sea air was cool on their cheeks as the girls moved to the edge of the deck and sat down along the railing; and in the distance, the albatross's high-pitched trills signaled the start of a new day.

The World Anew

S UNLIGHT GLITTERS BRILLIANT GOLDS and blues atop the undisturbed snow as we crest the hill. The sky is clear, yet clouds of steam appear in the air ahead of us, even through the thick wool scarves wrapped around our faces. My joints ache from the cold and from weeks of riding saddlesore. I'm dreading the shards of glass I will feel in the soles of my feet when I dismount for the day.

There are four of us who ride together now. None of us have shared names with each other—there is no need. In all the days and nights we've spent in this vast frozen tundra, we have seen no other living souls.

Not human ones, at least. There are, of course, plenty of other voices where ours have long been snuffed out. The distant bray of a moose occasionally carries over the hills as we walk. At night, the screams of foxes reach our ears. Once, as I moved along the forest, I even heard the low, grunting snuffles of a snout rooting through the snow. I didn't stay long enough to catch a glimpse of the round mass of brown fur I figured owned it; more importantly, I didn't stay long enough for him to catch sight of me.

And then there are our horses, blowing softly as their hooves crunch through the ice. The steam rises off their fur the same way it escapes from our breath. In the harsh, lung-aching chill and the stretches of blinding white landscape, it's become my favorite reminder that we have survived this long.

I have yet to encounter the wolves, and I wake each day praying that we won't. We know they're here—their paw prints leave indents in the snow that trace the borders of their territory. Their howls when pools of color dance in the dark sky deepen the chill in my bones, setting our horses on edge. The other riders feel it, too. One—the smallest of us, whose dark horse matches her own mane—I can see tense every time their cries reach our campsite. Her eyes widen, and she sits up straighter, pricking her ears toward the sound.

I think they've come for her before.

But today, there is nothing except the huff of breath from our horses, and the rhythmic squeaks and groans of the leather of our saddles as the weight of our packs and our seats shift. We are following the river, now frozen thick enough for us to ride across, to the shadow of trees in the distance. We tread carefully across the surface, the woman on the sorrel horse at the front of our group dismounting at one point to coax her mare through the safest path. We are patient with her; we know our roles in keeping her horse calm as much as she knows her own.

Once we're across, Sorrel remounts, and we draw nearer to the tree line. The woods are a promise of food and shelter from the wind, of the warmth of a fire—and they're also another chance for hope. I can't remember how long we've ridden, but we've followed the same river as it's traced through the landscape for weeks now, trusting it will lead us somewhere better.

And today, it has.

Not far into the trees, Gray hears rustling. She is our hunter, and as I turn back to find the source of the sound, already she has nocked an arrow and readied her bow. She raises it high and aims, firing just as I finally spot her target: a turkey roosting in a tree, several yards deeper into the forest. The bird falls, and Gray replaces her bow on her back, taking point to lead the group to our dinner.

But as we ride closer, our other senses awaken, and the smell of smoke wafts by our noses. We meet each other's gazes, at once confused and curious. As Gray dismounts to collect the carcass, she nods for us to ride on ahead, toward the scent.

It doesn't take long before we find the source of it. Sorrel halts, holding up a fist to signal to the rest of us to stop, then points at a small shape in the distance. I squint through the trees, but eventually I see it: a wooden structure, darkened to gray and black with age, a red chimney rising through the roof and spitting smoke into the clouds. Harnessed to its side is a water mill, frozen in place in the extreme cold, resting just on top of the surface of the river.

My gaze darts from the old cabin to the other riders and back again; I need to make sure they have seen the same thing. Bay holds a hand in front of where her mouth would be beneath her scarf, her eyes wide. As Gray approaches alongside us, Sorrel stands in her saddle, leaning forward to get a better look. The rest of us turn to her; as far as we can tell, she is the oldest and most experienced among us, and the closest we have to a leader.

She gives a slight nod, then urges her horse onward, and we follow suit.

As we near the house, the smell of smoke becomes stronger, and my heartbeat picks up. The fire that was here is recent. My horse starts to dance beneath me, bobbing her head and trying to drift out of line, wanting to canter ahead of the rest. She can sense my excitement, I know. I collect her reins and try to collect myself as well.

And then Bay makes a noise from behind me, a small strangled sound in her throat, and we all stop, turning to look at her. Her back is rigid, her eyes turned down to something in the snow. Gray raises a gloved finger and traces it out for the rest of us: lines of paw prints tracing up and down the riverbank. I follow them through the snow with my eyes, tracing their crisscrossing patterns all the way back to where my horse paws at the ground. I glance down by her hoof; there are a few drops of blood indenting the frosty surface.

Bay shakes her head, already turning back for the woods and urging her horse into a trot. I frown, raising my palm up to the sky, making the same motion as the curling smoke behind me. But the others just lower their gazes and follow the smallest rider. The world is no longer ours; it is theirs, and they've already claimed this territory as their own.

The sun is setting faster in the sky these days, so we waste no time in finding shelter for the night. As Gray readies the fire and our food, the rest of us tend to the horses, grooming them down and setting out water and forage, then raise the tarps and pelts for our own camp. We must act fast; the temperatures drop dangerously quickly as the sun dips in the sky, making our fingers fumble and our minds start to slow. A long time ago, before the other riders, I encountered someone who had waited too close to sunset and paid the price. As the sun had disappeared behind the horizon and the chill had soaked through his skin, his body had told him he'd started a fire when there was none. I found him the next morning, some feet away, his layers strewn out behind him. With his eyelashes frosted shut and a blanket of snow covering his shoulders, he looked peaceful, as if the world had tucked him in and kissed him good night.

The thought of that deadly kiss had seared itself into my memory, haunting me in all the years since.

I think of that kiss again now, as my lips grow slick with grease from the turkey meat. The food is warm and rich, and more than enough to fill my stomach. But there's a gnawing there, too—one that doesn't come from hunger. In the smoke from our campfire, I can see the curling gray tendrils rising out of the chimney earlier. And though another human, if they are there, may not await the same fate as the man I saw before, I can't help but feel guilty while we warm ourselves by the fire and fill our bellies with food. It's been some time since I traveled alone, but I remember the fear I felt when I saw that man and realized how easily he could've been me.

We rarely say much to each other, the other riders and I, but tonight, no one is even willing to meet another's gaze. Bay doesn't even wait for the coals to dim before she has curled up under her pelts and fallen asleep. Not long after, Sorrel banks the glowing embers that remain of our fire, and the rest of us turn in, bedding down in our layers of fur and wool. But as soft breaths and snores begin to fill our tent, I lie awake, my eyelids growing heavy but refusing to close.

I listen first to the snorts of one of the horses outside, to another nuzzling the hay and forage we left for them overnight. Then to an owl, much deeper in the trees, calling out in a series of low hoots.

Then, I listen to the wolves yipping in the distance.

I can't do it any longer. Slipping out from beneath my pile of bedding, I dress again in my outer clothes and boots, then duck out of the tent, heading toward the herd. I spot my horse's dapples easily in the moonlight, and she sees me as well. Her ears prick toward me as I approach; she senses something is different. I take only her bridle—bothering with anything else will take too long, and I don't need it, anyway—and slip it over her head. Before I mount, I also grab one more item from where our saddles lay on the ground: my utility knife. Just in case. I tuck it into the side of my boot and lever myself onto my horse's back in one fluid motion, and then we head for the frozen water mill just beyond the trees.

The night seems quieter on my horse's back, or maybe it's my thoughts that have been shushed. I feel at peace as her warmth seeps through my clothing and her scent, of hay and fur and dust, clings to my nostrils. Riding without a saddle, I feel her footsteps even more than usual, rocking with her every few steps as her weight shifts and she packs the snow down with her hooves. In this world, she is as dependent on my survival as I am on hers, but these are the moments where we are truly one.

Without warning, she stops, holding her head up high, her ears pricking forward toward a sound. I've not been paying attention, but she has; we've reached the edge of the tree line. Outside of the cover of the canopy, the sky is clear tonight, and the moon casts enough light to illuminate the structure from before.

My heart starts to pound. My horse shifts her weight, not sure how to interpret my nerves, though I'm not sure what to make of them either. I pause, adjust the reins in my hand, then listen. The wolves still sound far away. I see no new tracks in the snow. I force myself to take a breath, to quiet my racing thoughts, then urge us both onward.

Another set of tracks join our group's trail from before as my horse and I approach the building. Without the trees to insulate us, each crunch of the snow underneath us seems to echo across the landscape, the noise skittering across the ice in every direction. I fight the urge to hold my breath as we wrap around the corner where the giant wheel lies still, encased in glass. We pick our way along the long edge of the building, into the shadow of the chimney and to the next corner. And there, we stop.

We've reached the entrance.

I pause a moment, thinking my actions through before I follow through with them. I dismount. Icy shards travel through my legs as I land. I adjust the reins on my horse's back, looping them together in a quick knot that will keep them out of the way of her stepping on them. I don't want to tie her up; I know she won't wander far, and I'd rather her have the chance to run if she needs. I take one last survey of the endless tundra, ensuring we're alone, then turn toward the front door, picking my feet up high in the snow.

The door swings open on rusty hinges that barely hold it upright. They protest loudly with the movement. But once I step inside, silence engulfs me, the buffeting winds blocked from all sides. I hesitate a moment, looking around the room. It feels as if I've traveled back in time. I take cautious steps forward, the floor groaning in concert, toward the leather couch, the wooden coffee table, the threadbare rug. The couch is cracked, its stuffing starting to show. Tufts of the fluff float along the floor as if some animal other than me has already discovered it. But a coffee mug still sits undisturbed on the corner, the contents at the bottom of it turned to stains over the years. A door in one corner seems to lead to another half of the building, toward where the water mill connects, but a framed photo hangs on the wall across from me, in the direction of the chimney on the outside roof. I walk toward it, then through a doorway that leads to the next room.

It's a bedroom, and here there are disturbed sheets, and a long-abandoned nest of some creature made out of a blanket in the corner. In another corner, a pile of quilts conceals a vague set of shapes. A tuft of hair peeks through near the top of the pile. I turn away; I won't investigate further.

But on the next wall, near the pile of blankets, is a fireplace—and fresh soot lining the back of it. I crouch down, investigating the crumbled remains in the ashes. And then I spot the door on the other side of the room, hanging just slightly ajar, and the black boot prints that lead toward it.

I straighten, moving slowly, cautiously, toward the closet door. My palms are up, my footsteps soft. With a careful hand, I ease the door open slightly . . . and when I see what's inside, a warmth spreads in my chest and down to my fingers.

The survivor is young, smaller than even Bay, with wild eyes and long, unkempt hair. I can't tell if they are male or female, but the grime I see on their outer clothes tells me what I need to know most: that they are on their own. I wonder how long that has been the case.

Without thinking, I reach a hand out, and the survivor shuffles backward on hands and knees, into a pile of clothes on the floor of the closet. I close my eyes and sigh, then try again, crouching down to their level, then reaching up to lower the scarf that covers most of my face.

I am like you, I hope I've said.

But their fearful eyes still dart around in a frenzy. And then they land on something just over my shoulder.

I turn slowly, toward the large furry body creeping into the room. From where I crouch behind the bed, I can only see the massive paws pad against the ground, but I can hear snuffling in the pile of quilts. I reach for my knife and withdraw it from my boot, holding my breath.

The wood creaks as the paws move, and the snuffling stops.

A moment passes, and I peer under the bed. No paws. I stand up, carefully. Peeking over the bed, no wolf. I turn back to the survivor and nod. *It's safe.* I motion for them to follow, then watch, hope burgeoning, as the survivor moves hesitantly forward.

As silently as we can manage, we creep toward the exit. The wind picks up, biting through small gaps in the wood that have grown over so many years in the elements—but it seems to want to aid our escape. The creak of our footsteps is lost among the groans and shudders of the rest of the house. As we funnel ourselves into the main room once more, I can already feel my heart lightening. My mind drifts to those back at the camp, and how they will react to our new member. The horses will need to take turns carrying them on their backs—

A strangled sound interrupts my thoughts, and I spin back to the survivor. They point a shivering finger at a mark on the ground. The shadow of soot is faint, but it dots the floor haphazardly, doubling back on itself and looping around the room. I follow it with my gaze, tracing it until it trails off behind the couch. It doesn't continue farther.

I shift my weight back, as if to retreat, but my discovery has come too late. As if knowing he's been found, the furry mass takes a cautious step from behind the couch, his head hunched low. His coat is a brindled gray, only a shade darker than my horse's hide. He stares at us, unblinking, with orbs that capture the glow of the sunset glinting atop the snow. He is beautiful . . . as only the most deadly things are.

I stare back at him through narrowed eyes. My fingers curl around the hilt of my knife, and heat floods my body. But then a movement from farther back pulls my focus, just for a moment. And I see a second wolf, this one with rust tinging the gray in her coat, pace just inside the front entrance.

We're being hunted. The truth of it doesn't elicit anything beyond acknowledgement; the threat of the moment has already spiked my blood with adrenaline. We are in their territory, and separated from our herd. We're cornered. There are other windows and doors through which we could escape, I'm sure—but in the time it would take to find them and break past, the wolves' teeth would already be at our throats.

The world we live in is a harsh reality, and as I set my jaw, I realize my fate here will be yet another example of it. But as I move myself back, blocking the survivor in the hallway with my body, I feel no regret. My death will be no unfortunate accident, like that which befell the man I saw so long ago. I watch the gray wolf prowl toward me, the red wolf weaving its path closer to where I stand. As I raise my blade in front of my chest, I steel myself for the coming moments with the knowledge of who will ride in my place.

The moments never come. As the gray wolf closes in, a sharp whinny from just outside the house is echoed by a yelp from another member of the wolf pack. The wolves' focus shifts for just a second toward the door. In the space it leaves, instinct takes over. I run forward, scooping the coffee mug from the table and hurling it toward the nearest animal. It shatters just in front of his paws, and he skitters away, circling back toward his pack mate. The two face me again, their tongues lapping at the air as they pant. One of them yips, and I shout back, brandishing my blade and making myself as large as I can.

And then a sound carries on the wind through the open door, and my heart swells. It's an echo of my shout, and then a chorus of them, growing louder alongside the thunder of hooves on frozen ground. I yell again, watching the wolves' ears pin back and their tails tuck. I wave my knife in front of me and stand my ground as they pace in tight circles.

And from behind me, another shout joins the cacophony.

Our display must finally be more than the creatures anticipated; in a moment, they slink out of the door and dart away. Their barks and whines drift over the snow, fading back into the welcome silence of winter. And only then do I feel myself settle. I lower my hands, and my knees quiver as I turn toward the survivor behind me.

Another noise—the crunch of packed snow—comes from the entrance, and I tense once more, brandishing my blade as I turn toward the sound. Bay stands in the doorway, her palms raised in a show of peace. Finally, I let my knife clatter to the floor.

When we finally emerge from the house, the rest of my herd is waiting at the entrance. Sorrel's horse stamps a hoof as if in impatience or to ward off the numbing cold. Gray, still atop her horse, holds the reins of Bay's horse and my own. I rush toward them and bury my face in my mare's mane, welcoming her hot breath in my hair as she nuzzles me. As I run my hands along her sides and down her legs, I realize she has a small scratch on her back leg; but it is far from her heart. It will heal.

When I turn to the others, I realize their attention is on the newcomer, who is hugging their arms close to their chest and shying away from the others. I watch as Bay takes their hand, gently, then guides them toward her horse, setting it against her mount's muscular neck.

Once the wolves left, Bay and I took in the survivor's clothes in the daylight. Their outer clothes needed patches desperately, and their hat bore a moth-eaten hole at the temple. Their nose and the tips of two of their fingers had turned a shade of deep red from exposure. We took turns scouring the closet in the room for warmer layers, and now, they are nearly swaddled—but not enough to hide their smile.

My gaze drifts over the horses, steam rising from their backs, then lands on Bay, who's watching me wordlessly, her eyes curious. I know what it took for her to ride here—for all of them. All I can do is nod my thanks. She nods back, then returns her focus to the survivor, gesturing first to them, then to us, then to her horse.

Daylight is precious in this world, but we all gladly spend it waiting for the survivor to learn how to balance on the bay horse's back, then for Bay to gather the reins in her hand and lead her horse—and the rest of our herd—back to the campsite. As we leave the house behind, and I feel my mare's hooves carving a path in the snow beneath me, the cold aches deep into my bones, and my stomach growls, long having forgotten the meal from the night before. But all this reminds me that I'm alive. That *we* are alive.

The midday sun glints off the frost in my horse's fur and the icicles in the trees, and on the untouched drifts stretching out all around us. Although I can admit to myself I don't know what comes next, I know humanity's path forward is ours to write.

The world will be what we make it.

Acknowledgments

A POCALYPSE STORIES HAVE ALWAYS inspired me for the ingenuity of their characters and their messages of hope in the most harrowing circumstances. Some of the stories you've read in this collection were written long before the idea for this project. Some contain references to the people and stories in my life that taught me those lessons of tenacity and hope. (One started as blatant self-insert fan fiction for an apocalypse video game that shall remain nameless to avoid accidentally infringing on others' IP, but my friends and family can probably guess which one.) They all share the same message: As long as humans survive, humanity will, too.

True to any good post-apocalypse story, there were times I wasn't sure this collection would live to see another day. I owe the greatest thanks to the people who encouraged me to see it through to the end.

Mom and Dad, it would be impossible to thank you enough for the love and encouragement you've shown my writing throughout my life, but I will never stop trying anyway. Daniel, I truly believe your dinner conversation years ago about how our family would survive the zombie apocalypse was the beginning of my love for this genre. Thank you for all the kindling you've added to that fire over the years. Jessica, thank you for the café dates, ice cream runs, and car duets that sparked ideas for this collection and helped carry it to the finish line. And Matthew, thank you for inspiring me always. I would go through any apocalypse with you all—even if we wouldn't make it too long in some of them.

Peter, you were one of the first to hear about this book and have been one of its most steadfast supporters. Thank you for reading every story, cheering me through every rough patch, and celebrating this collection alongside me every step of the way. I love you to the end of the world.

Robyn Sarty, I truly could not have completed this collection without you. You demanded I keep writing, then demanded I keep rewriting, and each story has been made stronger because of it. I could not ask for a better accountability partner, beta reader, or friend.

An extra thank you to Daniel for turning my rambling descriptions into a cover that was worlds better than what I had envisioned, and to Abby Blenk, whose illustrations inspired so many stories for this collection when the book itself was still just an idea.

And you, reader—thank you for reading these stories and turning them into more than words on a page. Your support makes my world endlessly brighter.

NICOLE A. SCHROEDER is a storyteller at heart. Her love of words has stood fast through heaps of notebooks; countless sleepless nights spent reading as a child; hours perfecting sentences in various newsrooms in her home state of Missouri; three months surrounding herself with books as a publishing intern in London, England; and weekends sacrificed to penning her own works in the midst of it all. If she's not at her writing desk, you'll likely find her in the saddle or spending time with her family: her parents, her two younger brothers, and her younger sister, all of whom have been her best friends and biggest supporters since she first learned to hold a pencil.

To keep up with all her literary adventures, visit LostLibraryPress.com, or sign up for her newsletter at subscribepage.io/GdDwZF.